HOW TO MAKE FIREWORKS

1. Take one headstrong single mother who has sworn off relationships.

2. Send her crashing (literally!) into one very sexy, very single, laid-back cowboy.

3. Add heroine's endearing father and her adorable little daughter—both of whom are easily won over by the cowboy's charms.

4. Throw in the Shady Lady Ranch, complete with the cowboy's lovable—not to mention matchmaking—parents.

5. Place headstrong female and hunky cowboy under an irresistible Montana big-sky sunset—alone, of course!

6. Sit back—and enjoy!

Dear Reader,

I've never had a twin, but I can see how much fun it might be to have someone who looks just like you but leads a completely different life, a life you could share if the two of you decided to trade places for a while. For Mari Lamott, things are a bit more complicated than that, though. The heroine of Kelly Jamison's *The Law and Miss Lamott* has a twin who's nothing but trouble, so taking her place brings trouble in its wake. Of course, it also brings handsome detective Patrick Keegan—and getting together with a man that gorgeous is certainly worth a bit of trouble. Read this delightful book and see if you don't agree with me.

This month also brings the newest installment of award-winning Marie Ferrarella's latest miniseries, THE CUTLERS OF THE SHADY LADY RANCH. In *Will and the Headstrong Female* you can watch a rancher with a strong protective streak, Will Cutler, clash with an independent woman—Denise Cavanaugh—who comes driving into town intending to drive right out again once the carnival she runs is over. But somehow she ends up staying—and you'll be as glad as she is that she did.

Have fun with this month's selections, and don't forget to come back to Yours Truly next month for two more books about unexpectedly meeting—and marrying!—Mr. Right.

Yours,

Leslie J. Wainger

Leslie J. Wainger
Executive Senior Editor

Please address questions and book requests to:
Silhouette Reader Service
U.S.: 3010 Walden Ave., P.O. Box 1325, Buffalo, NY 14269
Canadian: P.O. Box 609, Fort Erie, Ont. L2A 5X3

MARIE FERRARELLA

Will and the Headstrong Female

SILHOUETTE **YOURS TRULY**™

Published by Silhouette Books
America's Publisher of Contemporary Romance

To
Anna Villareal,
with deepest regrets that it took so long

 SILHOUETTE BOOKS

ISBN 0-373-52079-4

WILL AND THE HEADSTRONG FEMALE

Copyright © 1998 by Marie Rydzynski-Ferrarella

Dear Reader,

I relate pretty strongly to the heroine in this story. Not that I've ever driven a big rig (in my case, the tinier the car, the better) or put together carnival rides (I draw the line at jungle gyms). But Denise is headstrong, and so am I.

Don't believe me? Just ask my husband...my kids...my brothers...my friends...my agent. I'm not ashamed of it. Being headstrong and stubborn has gotten me where I am today, with a career and a sexy husband I love. If you want it, don't wait for it to come to you. Go out and get it. You'll feel wonderful once you do.

Will Cutler did. Don't let his quiet exterior fool you. Quiet people can be just as stubborn as talkative ones. Will saw Denise Cavanaugh and decided she was the one for him. She had other ideas, but he refused to be put off. In essence, he "out-headstronged" her, and my hunch is that she'll be eternally grateful he did.

Hope this book brightens your day.

All my love,

Marie

1

Don't *you* be the one to miss out on Serendipity's Annual Carnival. Bring the whole family and stay the day. Dozens of rides and attractions await you.

Denise Cavanaugh's hands shifted slightly on the wheel of the big-rig she was driving as she glanced over to see her six-year-old carefully fold the flyer. It was going to be the latest addition in her collection. She had started the collection for Audra when her daughter was first born. Now that she was, in Audra's words, "a big girl," Audra kept up the collection herself.

There was a flyer from every single carnival and fair they'd hit. Right now, the flyers' main attraction were all the different pretty colors. In time, Denise was sure, the little girl would see the flyers for what they were. Memories. A road map detailing the path of their lives.

Tucking the flyer away under her seat, Audra impatiently began waving her short legs out in front of her.

"Are we there yet?"

The question wiggled its way in between the low, mournful words coming from the singer on the radio. It prevented Denise from being swallowed up by the almost hypnotic stupor that was threatening to engulf her at any moment.

Denise smiled at her daughter's question. A question probably echoed by children of all ages since before the first covered wagon had ever crossed over the Rockies. Certainly before the battered big-rig she was driving had traversed Route 12 from Wyoming, on its way to Serendipity, Montana.

Nostalgia whispered along the outskirts of her mind, softening her smile even further. Denise could remember a time, not really all that long ago, when she'd piped up with the same restless, eternal question, undoubtedly driving her father crazy.

Then it had been her father behind the wheel of the lead big-rig with her looking impatiently out the window, waiting for the world to have something to show her besides miles of open nothingness.

Denise glanced to her right. Now her father was in the passenger seat, looking out, with Audra sandwiched between them.

Maybe sandwiched wasn't quite the right word. Audra was slight for her age, as she had been. There was more than enough room for the six-year-old to sit comfortably, no matter how long the journey. But Denise knew that it wasn't lack of space that made her daughter so fidgety. It was the monotony of travel, of waiting to get somewhere. Anywhere.

Even traveling with a carnival could get old, if you did it all the time. They were like turtles, Denise mused. With their homes always at their backs. There was comfort in that. Immense comfort. This way, home was never far away. You always knew where to find it. But Audra was too young to understand that just yet.

She would, soon enough, Denise thought.

Denise let go of the wheel long enough to cover Audra's small hand with her own. She squeezed it gently.

"Almost, baby," she assured her. "We're almost there."

At least, she added silently, if her calculations were on target.

Audra wriggled, pulling her hand away. "Don't call me baby." Her lower lip stuck out in a petulant pout, negating the validity of her words. "I'm not a baby."

Denise tried very hard to erase the smile from her lips. Audra was in such a hurry to grow up just as she'd been when she was Audra's age. And she'd had a definite goal in mind. She had wanted to grow up to be a carnival performer. That was when there had been a carnival to perform in, before things began to fall apart.

"Sorry," she said in her best apologetic voice—a voice that was utterly fresh since she rarely apologized for anything. "I keep forgetting. You're an old lady of six now."

Denise caught her father's eye over Audra's baby fine blond hair and saw him wink at her. He was remembering, too, Denise thought. Remembering better times, when the two of them had ridden like this, with a full carnival behind them, not just the shell. But the carnival rides were all that was left of what had once been Cavanaugh's Carnival. The years and harder times had slowly stripped them of their family of performers until only this bare skeleton crew, the rigs they drove and the rides remained.

Like tiny nuggets of gold at the bottom of the miner's pan after the silt had been washed away. That's the way her father had described those who had remained each time their numbers shrank a little more.

Tate Cavanaugh was an incurable optimist. She, on the other hand, had been cured.

Royally.

The steady rocking rhythm of the cab as they drove made drowsiness difficult for Denise to fight off. She widened her eyes, willing them to stay in that position. Or, at least open.

Still, it was a good life, she thought doggedly as she gripped the large wheel harder. A good life with no boundaries to hem her in. And if she didn't like a place, well, they'd be someplace else soon enough. There was always someplace else.

That was what was so great about this country, Denise thought. Its endless supply of someplace else to be.

It was obvious that today, they wouldn't be there soon enough for Audra's taste. Denise glanced again at her fidgeting daughter. July was a bear almost anywhere. The heat and humidity was making Audra edgy.

It wasn't doing all that much for her, either. Denise sighed. She, too, wished that they were "there" already. Even with the windows in the cab wide-open, there was no relief. It felt as if the air had been packed in tight little boxes, all stacked up on her chest, all weighing heavily. And this last stretch of road before Serendipity seemed endless.

She jerked her eyes open again. Damn it, what was the matter with her?

"You look tired, Denise. Why don't you let me drive for a while?"

Denise slanted a quick glance toward her father. If she looked tired, Tate Cavanaugh looked even more so. Her father had been looking steadily more and more haggard as the months passed. There had to be something wrong for him to have allowed her to take over running the company. The shift wasn't anything that had been agreed to out loud, just something that had slowly evolved over the last six months. She did more and more, and he let her. The old Tate never would have allowed it.

But if she so much as said anything on the subject, or urged him to see a doctor, she was roundly put in her place and told that "Everything's fine. A man my age's earned the right to look a little tired now and then."

It wouldn't have bothered her if it had been "now and then." It was the constant that worried her. But worrying never changed anything and she knew it was useless to let the emotion get the better of her.

Most emotion was useless, she thought. Except for when it came to loving her family.

Turning to look at her father again, Denise did her best to sound blasé. "Not on your life. I've waited twenty-six years to get my hands on this wheel. I'm not about to let it go now. You had your turn, now it's mine."

"Mama, look out!" Audra shrieked.

The sudden, alerting cry jarred every single nerve in Denise's body. Almost subconsciously, she began turning the wheel sharply to the right even before she fully focused on the road.

And into the path of an oncoming Jeep.

Terror bit down hard.

"Oh my God."

Denise wasn't sure if the words had come out of her mouth, or were just thundering in her brain over and over again, like hail angrily pelting a tin roof. Along with the cry came fragments of prayers.

Tires screeched and whined as she fought not to jackknife the rig or hit the car that had, only a second before, not been there.

Had it?

Her arms and lungs were aching, straining against fear and steel. Sweat poured down her back, plastering her lime green T-shirt to her body. She turned the wheel into the skid, still praying. Forgetting the moment they were out of her mouth, she shouted words of reassurances to her father and daughter. All she was really conscious of was that their lives were in her hands. Hands that would have been trembling had they been free.

Five seconds felt like forever. Her daughter's cries and her father's voice assaulted her ears. None of it was intelligible to Denise. She couldn't make out any of the words. All she heard was the sound of fear.

And the pounding of her own heart.

Arms feeling as if they were about to break off, Denise was both exhausted and strung out by the time the big-rig finally screeched to a resounding halt. A lumbering dinosaur tired of the game.

Denise blinked back tears she didn't remember gathering in her eyes. It was over.

"Are you okay, baby?" she cried. Not waiting for an answer, she ran her hands over the girl's small body and face to reassure herself.

For once, Audra didn't object to the name. The golden head bobbed up and down.

"Uh-huh." Her mother's daughter, Audra stubbornly swallowed a sob, refusing to let tears fall. Tears were for scared babies. As long as Mama was there, everything was okay.

Pressing Audra to her, Denise raised her eyes to her father, almost afraid of what she would see. But he appeared to be unhurt.

"Daddy?"

The slumped figure straightened, pressing his shoulders against the back of the seat behind him. Tate shrugged away the concern he saw in his daughter's face.

"Shook up, some, but everything's where it's supposed to be." Tate let out a long breath, waiting for it and the pounding of his heart to become steady again. "Told you I should have taken over the wheel."

There was no accusation in his voice. There never was. Denise knew that right now, he was simply a parent who believed that he was omnipotent when it came to keeping his family safe.

She knew the feeling, except that for several very hairy moments, it had been snatched from her. But they were all alive and that was all that mattered.

The door of the cab suddenly flew open on her side. "Everyone all right in here?"

Startled, it was all that she could do not to jump in response. Heart still pounding, Denise turned from her family to look down into the face of a man with the most soulfully blue eyes she had ever seen.

The next moment, she braced herself for the tirade she knew was coming. They were the outsiders and she had almost run over someone she assumed was a "townie." Someone who belonged here, the way they didn't.

She pressed her lips together, eyeing him guardedly. "We're okay."

The woman was decidedly pale, Will Cutler thought. He had no idea who she was, or what she looked like normally, but he sincerely doubted anyone had a complexion quite that white. Small wonder. There had been several moments back there, after he'd swerved out of the way, when he thought the rig was going to wind up skidding along on its side. Or worse.

Scrambling to her knees, Audra peered around her mother's body to look at the stranger. Curiosity had been her constant companion from the first moment she'd opened her eyes. Now was no different.

"Yeah, we're okay," she announced, doing her best to sound just like her mother. The toss of her head was pure Denise Cavanaugh, even if she didn't have the long, flowing blond hair to carry it off.

Will looked from the woman to the little girl who was almost a complete miniature copy of her. He was only marginally aware that there was a third person in the cab, an older man who seemed content to let the females do the talking.

"Are you sure?" Will moved closer. He was about to climb up on the step, but the woman set her foot on it first, barring access. "No bumps or scratches?" His question was addressed to the little girl.

Pleased at the attention, Audra beamed importantly. "Nope. My mama's a great driver."

If the woman had been alert, she would have never crossed the dividing line and put them all in danger in the first place. But Will bit back the obvious comment. He wasn't the agitator in his family. That dubious honor had always belonged to his sister, Morgan.

"She'd have to be," he agreed solemnly, "to handle this rig."

Audra wiggled further forward, warming to the stranger like a match struck against a rough surface. And far too quickly for Denise's liking.

"I'm Audra Cavanaugh." She put her hand out the way she'd seen grown-ups do.

Amused, Will reached in over the woman to take the little girl's hand. He noted that the woman remained rigid and partially in his way, as if she intended for her body to act as a buffer between Audra and him.

"Pleased to meet you, Audra Cavanaugh. I'm Will Cutler." As he shook her hand, Will looked more closely at the last passenger in the rig's cab.

The older man looked thoroughly shaken. Will certainly didn't blame him. Though he probably didn't look it—his brothers and sister maintained that he had the emotional level of a clam—Will felt pretty shaken up himself. Before he'd swerved off the road, the rig had appeared to be coming straight at him. And after he'd gotten out of the way, he'd heard the little girl's scream above the screech of the tires. It didn't take an active imagination to envision the dire consequences that could have happened. He still carried vivid memories of the car accident that had snuffed out the lives of his two best friends when they had all gone joy riding in high school.

This had brought it all back to him. It had taken him a minute to collect himself before running to the rig to check on its occupants.

His gaze locked with the older man's. Of the three, he looked the worst. No cuts or bruises, but there was something in his expression, a look of pain he was attempting to conceal. Will wondered if the man needed medical attention.

"How about you, sir? Are you hurt?"

Denise could take care of her own; she didn't

need some stranger interfering. "You don't have to worry," she snapped. Her nerves felt more raw than gloveless hands in a snowstorm. Her tone brought the stranger's eyes back to her. "We're not about to sue you."

Tate knew that tone. Had lived with it for more years than he could recall. First his wife, Dierdre, now Denise. All the women in his family had tempers hot enough to fry bacon. Tate reached over and placed a long, thin gentling hand on his daughter's arm.

"Denise," Tate cautioned.

"Sue me?" Will echoed. He stared at her incredulously. "Lady, you were the one swerving into the wrong lane, not me."

As Denise shrugged off his hand, Tate leaned forward. "She apologizes, Mr. Cutler."

Being addressed as Mr. Cutler always made him feel as if he were masquerading as his father. He shook his head. "It's Will."

"I do not apologize," Denise hotly challenged.

No harm had come to the stranger. They had been the ones in danger from what she could see. Denise had always hated apologies. It was what you did when you didn't belong. As if not belonging to a permanent address made you a lesser person. Apologies gave the impression that you were humble, and she had no intention of being humble. Her father had been humble all his life, and all it had gotten him was stepped on.

Tate gave his daughter a halfhearted reproving look. He could never make her behave, even when she'd been a little girl.

"She's tired," Tate explained to Will. There was no reason to treat the man with hostility. After all, he had stopped to see if they were hurt and the incident had been Denise's fault whether she admitted it or not. Tate did his best to smooth over any feathers that might be ruffled. "We've been on the road since before dawn."

His eyes shifted toward the woman the other man had called Denise. "That would explain the testiness," Will allowed. The color was quickly returning to the woman's cheeks, chasing away the pale hue. She was beginning to look a whole lot better, Will thought. "Serendipity's only ten miles up the road. Maybe you'd better plan on stopping."

"We are planning on staying," Audra volunteered, eager to be part of the conversation.

Godfather to two of his friends' children and the oldest of five, Will knew how to talk to kids. He put the proper wonder in his voice to satisfy Audra.

"You are?"

"For two weeks," Denise added quickly. Audra's statement had made it seem as if they were moving in permanently.

Will looked at Denise. "You're coming for the carnival?"

"We *are* the carnival," Audra announced proudly.

Denise ran a hand over her daughter's hair. The note of pride in Audra's voice warmed her.

"She means we're responsible for the carnival rides," Denise explained. For a moment, her voice lost its testiness. She saw the stranger arch an eyebrow and look at the end of the rig. Denise could almost hear what he was thinking. The rig was big, but not that big. "The other trucks are on the road behind us. We went on ahead."

Will grinned. She came across a lot better when she wasn't behaving like a lioness, guarding her cubs. "Thanks for the warning."

The grin got to Denise far more effectively than his smile had. Guilt tweaked at her conscience. Maybe he wasn't so bad after all. She had jumped on him pretty hard, Denise thought. That was her way: pounce first, sort things out later if necessary. Sometimes, it was inappropriate.

Like maybe now.

Impulse had her jumping down from her seat in the cab. Instinct made her turn quickly, in time to keep Audra in place. Right now, she just wanted a moment with the man she'd almost run off the road.

Will stepped back as he watched Denise get down. She reminded him of Samantha, the Persian cat his mother had once owned. Samantha had the same way of unconsciously stretching her body, arching it gracefully whenever she jumped down from somewhere, or rose from her place. When he thought back on it, he vaguely remembered that in her own fashion, Samantha had ruled them all.

Will entertained the hunch that Denise Cavanaugh probably had that trait in common with Samantha, too.

Feeling a trifle embarrassed at the way she'd spoken to him, Denise extended her hand. "I didn't mean to be rude. It's just that—"

With a wave, Will dismissed the rest of her words and enveloped the long, slender peace offering with strong fingers.

"I understand," he told her warmly. "My life flashed before my eyes, too."

It hadn't, really, but it seemed to be the appropriate thing to say. If his life did flash before his eyes, Will figured it would be fairly dry, unemotional fare. His head would be filled with a myriad of sketches, both finished and unfinished, all of the buildings that had his mark on them. From the additions on his parents' ranch and the house that his brother Kent lived in right on up to the proposed tract going up on the outskirts of town as soon as the carnival ended.

Denise nodded, grateful that she didn't have to finish. It undoubtedly would have made her seem vulnerable to the man, and vulnerability was something else she didn't like to admit to. If you were vulnerable, that meant you immediately became someone's prey. That was something she vowed she was never going to allow to happen. At least, not again.

Still, she did want to make some sort of amends, seeing how decent he'd turned out to be about the near accident.

"Why don't you come by once the carnival is open?" Everyone in these small towns came to the carnival. It was practically the only sort of entertainment they had. Denise knew that from experience. The least she could do was treat him. "I'll leave a couple of tickets for you and your wife at the front gate under my name. Denise Cavanaugh," she repeated, in case he hadn't made the connection.

Cavanaugh. Like the sign on the truck. Will wondered if the man in the cab was her father or her husband. If he was the latter, it was definitely a May-December match. "In that case, then you'd better just leave one."

"You and your wife not speaking?" Tate spoke up, curious.

"Not yet," Will answered. A whimsical smile played on his lips as he looked back at Denise. "It's hard to speak to someone I don't know."

Audra's small, perfect features puckered as she

tried to understand what was being said. "You don't know your wife?"

Will laughed. Maybe he was being a little obscure at that. "No, I don't have a wife."

Audra's eyes lit up like Roman candles. "Mama doesn't have a husband."

Oh God, not again. Denise didn't know what had gotten into Audra, but in the past six months, her daughter had been trying to pair her off with every available man under seventy. Having her grandfather around suddenly wasn't enough for the girl.

But it was going to have to be. Denise tried her best not to look embarrassed. She flashed an annoyed look in Audra's direction.

"I'm sure Mr.—" Her mind a blank, Denise turned toward the man to refresh her memory.

The blush in her cheeks was turning to an interesting shade of pink. "Cutler," Will supplied, making no effort to hide his amusement.

Denise drew herself up, shoulders rigid as if she were a soldier just first entering battle. "I'm sure Mr. Cutler doesn't need to know that."

No, Will thought in silent agreement. He didn't need to know that she wasn't married. But all the same, he had to admit that it was definitely a nice piece of information to store away.

2

"So you'll come?" Audra looked up at him with hopeful eyes.

Will laughed at the unabashed innocent eagerness facing him. "I can't remember when a lady was so eager for my company."

He hadn't been to the carnival since he was a teenager. Life and issues that were far more important than carnivals and fun had gotten in the way. But his life was on track now, heading along in the direction he'd planned for himself. He'd been working for an architectural firm for four years now. In general, he supposed that things were going just about as well as he could ask for. Maybe it was time to kick back a little and learn about those flowers his mother was always telling him about. The ones by the wayside that he was supposed to smell.

"I wouldn't miss it for the world," he told Audra. He couldn't help but notice that the exchange between Audra and himself seemed to perturb Denise. What he couldn't quite get a handle on was why.

She'd been the one to offer the tickets in the first place.

Given the headway she'd made, and her nature, Audra pushed a little further. "Maybe you could even come to watch us set up? Mama never lets me do anything to really help. You could talk to me if you wanted to. Or help Mama," she added quickly.

He could have sworn that a sly look had crept into the little girl's expression. But the next moment, it was gone.

"Audra," Denise said sharply. Audra's friendliness was really getting out of hand. She didn't need some townie kibitzing and getting underfoot while they worked against time to set up the various rides and check them out. She gave Will a frosty, albeit apologetic, look. "I'm sorry, I don't know what's gotten into her. We don't need any extra help." Without thinking, she caught her bottom lip between her teeth, her mind on the unpaid bills that she had stored in the metal box in her trailer. The bills that were growing far faster than their proceeds these days. "Certainly none we could pay for, so if you're looking for a job…"

Will was aware that Denise was looking at his faded jeans and worn shirt. He'd spent the night at the Shady Lady, his parents' ranch, and was on his way home to change clothes before going into town and the office. He probably looked like a day laborer to her.

"No, no job. Just looking to be friendly, that's all." Drake Barkley, his partner on his latest project, had called to say the meeting with the developers about the proposed tract had been moved to nine. He'd already dipped heavily into his supply of time and needed to get going. Backing away from the rig, he nodded at Audra. "I'll see you at the carnival grounds, then."

"I'll be looking for you," Audra promised, calling after him. She covered her mouth and giggled when Will waved at her. Mischievous eyes looked up at her mother. "I like him."

That was the trouble. Audra liked everyone. And while she didn't want to squelch that wonderful innocence, neither did Denise want Audra to walk unwittingly into heartbreak the way she had because no one had seen fit to curb her friendliness.

Denise shook her head. "Audra Jean Cavanaugh, I don't know what's gotten into you."

Sighing, Denise climbed back into the cab and started the rig again. The engine rumbled to life, bringing with it another golden oldie. She slanted a glance at her side mirror. Denise could see Will walking back to his Jeep. No doubt about it, the man looked good—coming and going.

Not that that really mattered, she reminded herself abruptly, but she had to admit that a good view was a welcome sight from time to time.

"The child's only trying to make friends, Denise.

Something that wouldn't exactly hurt you to do, you know,'' Tate observed.

He wasn't lecturing her, he was only lamenting the fact that ever since that summer she had her heart broken, his daughter had changed. She'd lost not only her innocence, but her ability to see the positive side of life. He found the latter far more lamentable.

Denise merely shook her head. Familiar ground. Her father was the optimist in the family. It was up to her to deal with bills and reality.

"Got all the friends I need or want right here," Denise informed him as they hit the road again.

Will left his sketches on the presentation easel. Walters and Waters, the land developers who were presiding over this meeting, wanted to study them a little more fully. Everyone involved knew it was a mere formality. The deal was set. It was a given they had gone into the meeting with.

Opening his oversize portfolio, Will eased in his notes.

Ever since he could remember, he'd loved to design houses and then build them. At first, there had been just simple drawings, then he'd made that elaborate dollhouse for Morgan when she was ten. Morgan had used it to house her action figures. No prissy dolls for her.

He grinned to himself. They all marched to different drummers in his family. The tune his played was one that involved developing the land he found himself on. Will knew he had arrived when he had gone from building onto his parents' house to building a house for Kent to live in.

Where did she live when she wasn't driving a big-rig around the country?

Will smiled to himself. There it was again, that stray thought that kept reeling him back to the woman he'd met this morning. He couldn't seem to quite get her out of his mind. Not that she'd actually interfered with his thought process during the presentation. Iron Will his siblings called him. It wasn't always a compliment. He was nothing if not self-controlled.

Sometimes, he thought, maybe just a tad too self-controlled. Of late, he found himself envying two of his younger brothers. Hank and Kent had each recently become seriously involved with a woman and now it looked as if both brothers were altar-bound.

Damn, but the world was a surprising place. Who would have ever thought that Hank would actually settle on one woman, or that one woman would actually put up with Kent and his single-minded ways?

Single-minded. The phrase made him think of Denise again. He'd be willing to bet that she was stubborn clear down to the bone. There was something about the set of her chin, the look in her eyes, that told him she was accustomed to getting her own way. And probably not because she was spoiled or indulged, he thought, but because she felt her way was the right way, the way that needed to be followed in order to get things done. The only way.

Will's mouth curved. He knew all about that. Knew all about having a set idea of how things were supposed to be done. As the oldest Cutler sibling, he'd had to make sacrifices to accommodate and help care for his brothers and sister. And to help out on the ranch. The Shady Lady was finally turning a nice profit, but it hadn't always been that way. Matter of fact, it had rarely been that way despite all the hard work that had been put into it. A large chunk of that burden had fallen to him.

Not that he minded, but there were times when Will felt as if his childhood had been indefinitely put on hold where it had remained until it eventually evaporated.

Every now and then, especially lately since his brothers were pairing up, he found himself wondering what he'd missed and yearning to find out before he was too old to enjoy it.

Maybe it was just spring fever, arriving a little bit late.

Drake rounded the large rectangular conference table and clapped a hand on Will's back in easy camaraderie.

"That went well, don't you think?" Drake deliberately kept his voice low, not wanting to attract undue attention.

Will zipped his portfolio closed again. In his estimation, Walters and Waters had been extremely receptive to the six different models he'd presented today. Their approval was the last necessary step before building could begin.

Will moved his portfolio off the table. He glanced back at the development company's representatives. "Yeah, it did."

Drake picked up on Will's tone. "You don't sound very happy about it."

Drake had caught him in an unguarded moment, Will thought. He'd designed a great many homes and buildings in his four-year career. The ones that were erected in the hearts of thriving cities never troubled him, but he always came away with ambivalent feelings when it came to building in Serendipity. It was different here.

"I am, but I have to admit, I wouldn't be my father's son if part of me didn't feel kind of sad to see that section of land go."

"It's not as if that was the last piece of undeveloped property in Montana. Or even the last with a spectacular view," Drake said.

Which Mountain Streams, the proposed residential tract, had in spades. The whole development had an awe-inspiring view of the mountains. Will knew he should be proud of his work, and he was, but there was that unmistakable tinge of sadness hanging around, as if, in building, he was also destroying something.

Pushing the conference room door open, he walked outside. Drake had to hurry to keep up.

"I know," Will agreed, "but the first settlers in Kentucky probably said the same thing when they built that first log cabin beside the Cumberland. It didn't look like an invasion then, but now look. You practically have to make an appointment to visit nature." Will looked at his friend. Drake didn't have a clue what he was talking about, Will thought. "We all lose a little bit of nature with every tree that gets cut down."

Will'd totally lost him. Drake began to wonder if maybe Will shouldn't start taking some of those vacation days he'd accumulated. "There're no trees, it's a field, remember?"

Will lifted a shoulder, then let it drop. Maybe he wasn't making that much sense right now. Maybe it was something else that was nagging at him. "Just making a general point, Dray."

Drake placed a hand on Will's arm, stopping him. "God, you're not turning into a mountain man on me, are you?" His brows narrowed as he scrutinized Will. "You saw *Centennial* on the cable channel again, didn't you?" It was an accusation. "You know what happens to you when you watch that."

Will laughed, his mood lightening a little as he

walked outside the building and to the parking lot. "No, I was just thinking that this time next year, the carnival won't be able to set up there." Suddenly, he regretted that he'd never made the time to go to the carnival before.

Drake still didn't see why Will didn't feel like celebrating. "So? It'll set up somewhere else. For crying out loud, Will, you're an architect. You build things. Damn pretty things." He squared his shoulders, as if bracing himself. "And if you start reciting 'I think I'll never see anything as pretty as a tree' again, I swear I'm going to seek psychiatric help for you."

A smile lifted the corners of his mouth. "You just butchered that line, you know." Will stopped beside his car, wrestling with his thoughts. It was a short round. He tossed his portfolio onto the passenger seat. "I'm not going back to the office."

Wary, Drake asked, "Why not?"

He tried to make it sound nonchalant, for his own benefit as well as for Drake's. "I've got some time coming to me. I think I'll take the rest of the day off and go to the carnival grounds. Tell Carter I had some personal things to attend to." High on the smell of triumph, Will knew his boss wouldn't mind him not coming in.

Will was making less and less sense to Drake. "There're nothing but squirrels running around there now, Will."

He thought of Audra, looking up at him with supplication in her eyes. And of Denise, who had a very different look in hers. Different but damn enticing, nonetheless.

He laughed, getting behind the wheel. "Well now, there's where you're definitely wrong."

Drake was left standing in the parking lot, looking at the back of Will's disappearing Jeep. "I hope so, Will. I sure hope so."

It was hard for some people to look at the barren tract of land, pockmarked with weeds and envision the houses that were to be. Will had no such difficulty. All he had to do was think about them and the houses seemed to rise up before his eyes.

But he wasn't thinking about the development-to-be when he drove his Jeep onto the area that would, in a matter of a couple of days, be roped off as the carnival's parking lot. He was thinking about all the carnivals that had been here before. And all the carnivals that wouldn't be here in the future.

Maybe it wasn't the development that was bothering him, he thought, maybe it was the idea of change. Despite his chosen profession, he'd never really been one for change. And things around him were suddenly changing rapidly.

If he thought about it, it seemed to him that so much of Serendipity was changing. It was far from large by big city standards, but he could remember

Main Street when it had only three stores on it and it wasn't the main street—it was the only street. The town had been named Serendipity because that was the feeling it generated if you should happen to wander into it. But now it was finally growing. Bit by bit, nature was giving way to civilization.

And he was helping that come about. He supposed he liked to feel that his designs made the transition more esthetically pleasing, but pleasing or not, there was no arguing with the fact that he was still bringing the changes about.

He wondered if he should be applauded or damned for that.

Even his family was changing. His brothers were getting married, probably starting families of their own in the future and for the first time, Will felt as if he was really left standing on the sidelines. He'd always been a player before, most of all in his family. A main player.

This was a turn of events he was going to have to work on to make right, he mused. And he'd better do it fast. Hank and Fiona's wedding was less than a month away.

Climbing out of the Jeep, he shut the door. If he were being completely honest with himself, he wasn't exactly sure just what made him come here. It certainly wasn't because of any encouragement, silent or otherwise, he'd seen on Denise's part. If he'd read her right, she would just as soon he didn't come wandering by while they were setting up. The invitation was for when the carnival was up and running, not before.

Maybe he was just trying to recapture that lost youth he'd been thinking about. Or maybe it was a sense of guilt that compelled him to come here, to absorb the area as it was before it changed.

Or maybe it was a woman with flashing blue eyes, a firm chin and an independent attitude.

Will shoved his hands into his pockets, crossing to where he saw activity going on.

"I've been waiting."

The voice, with its little old lady intonation, made him smile even before he turned around to look down at Audra. She was standing behind him, her hands fisted on her small hips and her booted toe tapping on the dirt. Undoubtedly mimicking her mother, he thought.

He could feel amusement taking hold. "You were that sure I was going to come?"

A smile broke out and before he realized it, Audra launched herself at him. He barely had time to drop to one knee and make the catch. Looking contented, she wrapped her arms around his neck. A warm feeling slipped over him. What would it be like, he wondered, to have one of these to come home to every night?

"Uh-huh, I was that sure. Wanna see what they're doing?" She pointed toward the grounds. It looked like the aftermath of a storm, with the skeletal components of rides fanned out in all directions. "I can 'splain things if you want."

He bet she could, too. He'd been around enough children to know that some came equipped with souls that seemed to have been born old. He'd had one himself.

Will tried to look properly solemn for Audra's benefit as he nodded. "I'll be sure to direct all my questions to you if I have any."

He had the oddest feeling that he was being watched. Turning, with Audra still in his arms, he saw Denise standing in the distance, looking in his direction. Even at that distance, their eyes met.

"There's your mom." He pointed toward Denise. "She doesn't look very happy."

Audra sighed mightily, as if she knew and it troubled her. "She's not. Mama's always worried about something."

Feeling he'd make faster progress if he carried the child, Will crossed to where Denise was standing. "What is she worried about?"

"Grampa's not feeling well, and Harry left this morning," she recited.

"Harry?" Was that the name of someone who was figured significantly into Denise's life? If he was, maybe his departure could explain the woman's testiness this morning.

Audra nodded, obviously enjoying imparting information. "Uh-huh. He took care of the merry-go-round for Mama." She looked sad. She'd liked Harry. He told funny stories. "He said he was tired of running around all over the place and he was going home."

"I see." The complaint was easy enough to understand. What was hard to understand was how a woman like Denise Cavanaugh could be content with this kind of nomadic life, even part of the time. "Where's home for you?"

In response, Audra pointed to the trailer behind him. "There."

He'd forgotten how literal children could be. "No, I mean when you're not traveling around. When you're not on the road."

"But we're always traveling around," she protested. "That *is* home."

Was it possible that she was right? That they went from one place to another twelve months out of the year instead of just six to nine?

Denise looked at him sharply as he approached. "Change your mind about suing?"

He placed Audra on the ground. He found he couldn't read Denise's expression. It was impossible to guess if she was kidding or not.

"No, I decided to take your daughter up on her invitation and come by." He gestured toward the line of bulldozers that stood off to the side, silent yellow sentry that were a constant reminder that this was the carnival's last year in this spot. "I guess I just wanted to look around before the bulldozers started their work."

A black look entered Denise's eyes at the mention of the vehicles. In the last few years, it seemed to her that more and more carnival grounds were disappearing. The number of carnivals taking place was shrinking. It was no easy feat to constantly keep coming up with new places to go so that their income didn't shrink along with the grounds. Right now, with competition coming from the other companies that found themselves in the same situation, they were just a shade over breaking even. They needed more than that to remain in business.

"You mean destruction, don't you?"

He'd hit a nerve, Will thought. What would she say if she knew he was directly connected to that destruction?

"Bulldozers?" Audra echoed in a voice that was properly appalled. "You mean we're not having a carnival here after all?"

He shifted uncomfortably at the look Denise gave him. "I'm sorry, they're not breaking ground until after you leave," he told Audra. "I didn't mean to give you the wrong idea."

"There's no right idea about bulldozers," Denise informed him tersely. "They come in, tearing up the grounds, making way for foundations of an army of houses or office buildings, all of them squatting on land like so many eyesores.''

No, she definitely wouldn't take to the idea that his signature was on those squatting eyesores, Will decided. For now, he wouldn't mention it.

"Well, not all of them," he argued.

Denise tossed her head, her hair flying over her shoulder. "Never saw a house I liked better than an open field.''

That wasn't strictly true, she amended silently. She had seen one. The house that had belonged to Audra's father. David Donnelly had belonged to another world, the so-called right side of the tracks. And he had the castle to go with it.

At least, it had seemed like a castle to her when she'd seen it. He'd seduced her there, simultaneously introducing her to heaven and hell at the same time. It had been heaven to be in his arms, and hell to discover that it hadn't meant anything to him— certainly not the way it had to her.

She'd been born on the road, just as Audra had, and had never known anything more than a couple of rooms in a motel and even those were sporadic and temporary.

You could have your houses, she thought. She'd take the open road every time.

Suddenly it became important to him to have her change her opinion. Whether to assuage his conscience, or just because he didn't want her thinking this way, he didn't know. "Maybe I could show you a few to change your mind."

"I doubt it." Leaning over, she took Audra by the hand. "Well, if you'll excuse us, we have work to do."

Audra's face lit up. "Me, too, Mama?"

She'd been younger than Audra when she had begun pitching in. There was nothing to be gained by babying Audra. Besides, if she was busy, maybe Audra wouldn't keep trying to match her up with men.

"Well, with Harry gone, I've shifted things around a little." She smiled down at Audra. "You can be in charge of hosing down the carousel horses, and then polishing them."

Audra's eyes gleamed. At last, she had a big people job.

"Heard about you losing a man."

Turning, Denise raised an eyebrow at the wording. "I didn't lose a man, he decided that he wanted to do something different with his life. His choice."

She was touchy about that. Had Audra's father walked out on her? Will didn't know why, but he'd just assumed the man had died. If he'd left her, that might explain her less than friendly attitude toward men. "I'm free for the afternoon if you need an extra set of hands."

Instead of taking or declining his offer, Denise took his hands in hers and examined them, first on one side, then the other. There were calluses on his palms. Always a good sign. Suddenly aware that she was holding them, she dropped his hands.

"What do you do for a living?"

The slight crimson tinge on her cheeks was becoming. "I build things."

She cocked her head, suspicion entering her eyes. "What kind of things?"

"Buildings." It was a cagey answer and he watched her face for a reaction.

"You're a carpenter?" Why was he being so guarded? Denise wondered. Was there something he was trying to hide? Just what sort of things did he build?

"In a way," he allowed.

He was definitely hiding something, she decided. "In what way?"

Evasion had never really been his way and it didn't feel right now. "I'm an architect."

"That's pencil and paper." She looked down at his hands again. Why did an architect have calluses? "Just how big is the pencil you push?"

He laughed and managed to coax a half smile from her as well as a giggle from Audra. "I believe in hands-on experience."

She was wasting time standing here, talking. "I can't pay much."

Was that what was bothering her? "I'm not asking to be paid." He looked down at Audra and winked. "I'm volunteering."

There had to be a catch. Didn't there? "For free?" Denise asked.

He spread his hands, as if to show her that he was hiding nothing. "For free."

"Well, that's the right price. C'mon, let's see about getting you a change of clothes and then putting you to work." Turning on her heel, she led the way to her trailer.

Standing on her tiptoes, Audra covered the side of her mouth and said in a loud whisper, "You'll like working for Mama. Just nod when she raises her voice."

Too bad Denise didn't have some of her daughter's charm. "Does she raise it often?"

"Uh-huh." Audra's golden head bobbed up and down. "But only when she's mad. Or worried," she added as an afterthought.

Denise turned around to see them lagging behind. And whispering. Now what?

"Audra..."

"Or calling me." Audra grinned at him as she pulled her hand from his and ran off to catch up to her mother. "I'm coming."

Watching them, Will had to wonder who ultimately was the bigger handful—the mother or the daughter.

3

Pulling off her work gloves, Denise shoved them into her back pocket. After almost three hours of hard labor, the area was finally beginning to bear some resemblance to a carnival.

"Want a soda?" Coming up behind her, Tate held out a can to his daughter.

"Thanks." She took it from him gladly. "As long as it's wet and cold, I don't care what it is."

Denise pressed the can against her forehead and then her throat before popping the top and drinking deeply. She hadn't realized just how thirsty she was until this minute.

Pausing, she looked over toward the carousel, where Will was now working with Skip and Tim. Before that, he'd helped fit the giant slide together with Roy and Cecil. She'd known exactly where Will was every minute of the last three hours. She'd kept tabs, expecting him to flag at any minute and withdraw his offer to help. He hadn't. He'd taken on one job after another, working as if he enjoyed it. As if his livelihood were coming from erecting these metal giants.

She couldn't figure him out.

Well, she had to admit he wasn't afraid of work. She also had to admit that he was very easy on the eye to watch while he worked. Her father's shirt was a little tight on him and she could see every muscle straining as Will helped lift and fit the horses into their proper positions. Without realizing it, her grip tightened on the can, indenting it slightly. She forgot to drink.

Tate grinned. He knew exactly where she was looking. "Works hard," he commented.

Caught, she shrugged indifferently as she looked away. "For an outsider."

He'd heard her use the term often enough, and it had begun to worry him. His once outgoing, gregarious daughter was withdrawing more and more from everyone outside their small, ever shrinking, tight circle. That wasn't a good sign.

"You know, Denny, not everyone who doesn't travel with us is an outsider."

Denise tossed her head, sending her hair flying over her shoulder. She drained the can in a last, long gulp, then crushed it. "Yes, they are. They're outside and we're in."

"Did you ever stop to consider that it might be the other way around?"

She stiffened at the sound of Will's voice behind

her. She hadn't heard him approaching. Denise glared at her father. He might have at least warned her they weren't alone. Handing the misshapen can back to Tate, she turned around to look at Will.

Tate knew when to withdraw from the line of fire. It seemed a good idea to pull up stakes now, so he did.

Like a bantam-weight fighter, Denise balanced herself on the balls of her feet, her face pugnaciously turned up to his.

"Meaning?"

She looked ready for a fight, he thought, and all he'd done was make a comment. "That you're the one on the outside?"

That was exactly the way she'd felt when she thought herself in love with Audra's father. At the time, being an outsider had stung and stung badly. Eventually she'd gotten over it and shored up her beaches.

But there was no reason to share that with this man.

Denise lifted her chin. "No, I'm the one who's free." Deliberately moving him out of her way, she strode toward the fun house. Even from here, she could see that the sign hanging over the top of the doorway was crooked. As she walked, she shoved her gloves back on her hands.

"Now if you've had enough slumming," she said dismissively, "you can go anytime."

It took a second for the verbal thrust to penetrate. He'd worked as hard here as any day he'd put in on the ranch. She had no right to be snide with him, especially since he was doing her a favor.

"Is that what you think I'm doing?" Annoyed, he caught up to her in three strides and turned her around to face him. "Slumming?"

Shrugging his hand off her arm, her eyes dared him to tell her differently.

"Aren't you?" She turned her back on him again, walking quicker this time. "Aren't you here just to get a kick out of this? See what it means to really work for a living instead of sitting back and not even breaking a sweat over what you do?"

It amazed him to feel anger forming in response to her accusation. He was the calm one in the family, the one who never lost his temper. But for some unknown reason, this slip of a woman with the rattlesnake tongue set him off.

"That's so wrong, I don't even know where to start untangling it."

She spared him one cold look over her shoulder before she went to commandeer a ladder. If he'd come expecting her to be grateful that a townie had spared a few hours to share some of their sweat, he was going to go away disappointed.

"Then don't bother."

Will glanced toward the rear lot where his Jeep was. For two cents he'd just walk away and...

Hell, this would bother him all night. Longer. He wasn't going anywhere until he put this foul-tempered woman in her place.

He caught Denise by the shoulder just as she began to drag the ladder back toward the "building" that had taken three of her crew the entire time to reconstruct.

"Just what the hell set you off?" Will demanded. "The fact that you're not right?"

This time, when she jerked her arm, he held fast. She struggled for a moment, then stopped. Her eyes narrowed as she looked at him. "What do you mean?"

Will realized that he was holding on a little too hard and dropped his hand. "You probably thought you had me pegged as some well-off snob—"

A smug smile curved her mouth. "Well?"

He felt a distinct desire to wipe that smile off her face, using any means possible.

"It depends on your definition of well-off, and I've never been accused of being a snob in my life." He caught the frayed ends of his temper before they unraveled completely and lowered his voice. "And I think that after about three hours of this, even you'd admit that I've held my own."

Maybe. To someone else. But not to him. "I don't have to admit anything," Denise said.

Why was he even bothering? If Will thought about it for any length of time, he didn't even know what he was doing here. If he was so all-fired bent on physical labor, he could have been putting the time in on his parents' ranch, not here for some ungrateful hellion.

Disgusted with her and himself, Will shook his head. "No, you don't. People like you never do."

He couldn't have annoyed her more if he'd deliberately tried.

"People like me," she echoed. Hands on hips, Denise glared at him. "Just what do you mean, people like me?"

"Prejudiced people."

"Prejudiced?" She stared at Will as if he'd lost his mind. How could he possibly accuse her of that? The crew that worked for her was as diverse a mixture of people as could be hoped for. One glance, however cursory, was all that was necessary to make him aware of that fact. "Boy, are you ever off. I don't have a prejudice bone in my body."

He managed to get a good portion of his temper under control, though not all of it. "Take another inventory. Somewhere amid that lovely bone structure of yours is a whole slew of prejudice bones."

She opened her mouth to retort, but he never gave her the chance. Years of surviving with Morgan had sharpened his reflexes and taught him to be quick.

"What? You think that you can only be prejudiced against color or religion? Well, think again." He could feel his temper reheating, fanned by his own words. "Lady, you think you have me all fig-ured out and stuck into some round little hole." One by one, he pointed out her flaws. "You're preju-diced against anyone who doesn't belong to your tight little group, you're prejudiced against anyone who you think has more money than they can keep in a sock and you're especially prejudiced against men."

There were a whole host of names that begged to be flung at him and she could barely contain them. But Audra was somewhere within earshot, and she wasn't about to let her daughter hear her swear at this pompous, muscle-bound jerk.

Instead Denise seasoned her response with smug sarcasm. "All this in three hours?"

He satisfied himself, for the moment, with an im-age of his hands around her slender throat. "I'm a fast study."

She wasn't rattling him—and that annoyed her beyond words. Her eyes became small, accusing slits. "Well, you're wrong on all counts."

How could he want to wring her neck one second, and desire her company the next? He wasn't on medication and as far as he knew, hadn't ingested anything to make him crazy. Yet there were these two very vital juxtaposed thoughts and feelings crashing into one another within him.

"Prove it."

Suspicion leaped up to take possession of Denise. "How?"

She was looking at him as if she expected him to turn into some mythical monster, Will thought. "Have dinner with me tonight."

Right, waltz into his lair, just like that. *Been there, done that.*

"The hell I will." She bit off the words, turning her back on him and grabbing hold of the ladder.

When he tried to help her with it, she blocked him with her body. The woman was impossible.

So why did he find her so damn compelling?

"All right, dinner with my family, then."

"Family?"

The word stopped her in her tracks. She looked at Will curiously. David had made excuses when she'd asked to meet his family. If she'd been seeing clearly instead of through rose-colored glasses, she would have realized that he was ashamed of her. All the signs had been there.

Now this man she cared nothing about wanted to drag her off to meet his people.

"My parents," he explained. "Maybe one or two of my brothers if we can scrounge them up." A smile played on his lips. "Bring Audra and your father along if you don't trust yourself."

Trust herself? What, did he think she was going to jump his bones? The smug bastard thought a lot of himself, didn't he?

"What are you talking about?"

The woman was almost shooting lightning bolts at him with her eyes. He began to enjoy himself. "Denny, I've learned that when there's this much feeling about something, the bottom line is passion."

Releasing the ladder, she turned to face him, raising herself up on her toes. "You're out of your mind."

Will merely smiled. "Am I?"

He was standing much too near for comfort. And his mouth was a great deal closer than she would have liked. She struggled, not with him but herself, because suddenly she was tempted. Tempted to see if those lips of his were as unsettling as his rhetoric was.

Maybe he was right. Maybe the bottom line was passion. But it wasn't what he thought. The passion was tied in with the very passionate desire to keep the lines between them straight, the boundaries all in place, and her small world unthreatened by anything that could throw it on its ear—the way it had once been when she fell for Audra's father.

For the first time in his life, Will struggled with the desire to sweep a woman into his arms and kiss her. It left him a little shaken. If he didn't know better, he would have said Hank was channeling through him. Hank was the ladies' man, not him.

He cleared his throat. "So what do you say?"

Staring into his eyes, she'd lost the thread of the question. "To what?"

"Dinner for openers."

Like a woman watching someone else's dream, Denise felt his smile curl its way into her system. Heard herself answer without remembering having formed the words. "I say okay to dinner and it's not an opener."

She was wrong, it was definitely an opener. "There you go again, being prejudiced."

Denise reconnoitered. "No, I'm being sensible. And there are lines—"

He could have sworn he saw a flicker of fear in her eyes just then. But that was impossible. What could she possibly have to fear from him? "Denny—"

Her back went up. "Don't call me that. You have no right to call me that."

He could only shake his head in wonder. "I have to earn the right to call you by your nickname?" He'd heard her father call her that. "You come with a lot of rules, lady."

She'd had enough of this. There was still a great deal of work to do. It wasn't going to get done by her wasting time, talking to him. Turning, she went up the rungs quickly.

"Then don't bother playing."

Annoyance bred a quick retort. But it dried up on

his tongue as, looking up, Will found himself staring at a very shapely posterior.

All right, maybe he'd stay in for another hand, he relented, although heaven only knew why. He wasn't the type to be reined in by flashing eyes and skin the color of freshly warmed bread, done to perfection. He didn't get swayed by physical attributes, never had. He'd always been far too sensible for that.

But there was something there, in those eyes of hers, that made him hang around for just one more exchange, one more rapidly fired volley. Something. He didn't explore it any further than that.

"You really want that?" he challenged, his voice suddenly low. "You really want me to 'stop playing' and go?"

His question made her realize that she was torn. And because she was, self-preservation took over and she lashed out. Hands curling around the rung, she swung her head around to look down at him, an emphatic "yes" hovering on her tongue. The ladder wobbled, and she overcompensated by shifting to the other side.

The ladder pitched backward. Denise swallowed a scream as she felt herself falling. The next moment, strong, hard arms were closing around her as the ladder clattered to the ground. Without thinking, she threw her arms around his neck, her body firmly pressed against his chest. Warmth penetrated, blanketing her fear.

Her heart hammered in her throat, making it almost impossible for her to catch her breath. When she finally did, she exhaled in an exaggerated huff to hide how shaken she really was.

Despite the thrust of the sudden drop, she hardly felt as if she weighed anything at all. Will smiled at her. "I guess it's a good thing for you that I didn't leave when you wanted me to."

Aware that her arms were still around his neck, she pulled them back and splayed her hands against his chest, pushing him away. It felt as if she were pressing against a rock.

Her eyes flashed a warning in self-defense. "If I hadn't turned around to answer you, I wouldn't have fallen off."

He entertained the idea of dropping her before deciding against it. One of them had to remain civilized. "Anyone ever tell you that you have the disposition of an angry hornet?"

Despite the flare of anger, Denise could feel her mouth curving at the absurdity of the situation. "Not anyone who's alive to tell about it."

Her hint of a smile coaxed a larger one from him. His temper vanished. "That sounds strangely like a threat."

Denise didn't want him holding her. It was far too easy to let herself like it. The struggling smile faded, replaced by a scowl. "Are you going to hold on to me like this all day?"

The woman's mood swung back and forth faster than a weather vane in a storm, Will thought. "No, eventually you'd get to be too heavy." Before she could say anything else, he set her down, then dusted off his hands. "So how about it, are you game?"

The fall had temporarily knocked everything out of her head. Everything, except that a woman could easily lose herself in a pair of arms like that—provided she hadn't already been kicked in the teeth by life.

"For what?" she asked suspiciously.

"Dinner," Will prodded patiently.

One shoulder rose, then fell carelessly as she looked off toward where the Ferris wheel was being set up. "I can't speak for my father—"

"Since when?" Will hooted.

The jeer brought her up sharply. Her fighting spirit returned. "What do you mean?"

She couldn't even manage to pull off that innocent act. "I wasn't just working these last few hours, I've been watching you. You order everyone around, your father included."

Watching? He'd been watching her? Why? Flustered, she tossed her head defensively. "I don't order, I...lead."

"Uh-huh." The grin on his face told her he

wasn't buying into her denial. "So lead them to the table."

She neatly changed routes. "You're awfully free with your parents' hospitality."

Oh, no, she wasn't going to wiggle out of it that easily. "So are they," he assured her. Will looked over toward the slide he and a burly crew member by the name of Cecil had put together. Cecil had tested it out three times before pronouncing it safe. Will figured if it could support a man who looked as if he outweighed the average family, it would support small children. Eager to test it out, Audra was flying down the silvery incline, a commando yell emitting from her lips.

Probably something her mother taught her no doubt, he thought.

He jerked a thumb at the child. "How long since she's had a home-cooked meal?"

Denise immediately read the negative side of the question. "Are you saying I can't cook?"

He couldn't picture her in a kitchen of any sort. He had a great deal less difficulty picturing her in his bedroom, maybe just dressed in her work gloves. The image coaxed an appreciative, sensual smile from him.

"Can you?" he challenged.

As far as cooking went, she didn't burn water, but she didn't exactly do very much else with it, either. "I don't get any complaints," she sniffed.

The nonanswer told Will all he really needed to know. "That's probably because they're afraid to complain."

She took offense at his inference. "My family's not afraid of me."

Maybe afraid was the wrong word, but he bet they knew better than to oppose her. "A benevolent dictator is still a dictator."

She didn't like what he was saying, even if the words were coming out of a firm, wide mouth that seemed to unsettle her every time he was close to her. "What's that supposed to mean?"

She knew damn well the way her family reacted to her, he judged. Knew, too, the kind of woman she was. Strong-willed to a fault. He was beginning to suspect that, in a one-on-one contest, she could put Morgan to shame.

"You're a bright lady, you figure it out. In the meantime, come to dinner."

"Why?" So he and his family could feel superior? So they could feel magnanimous, extending charity in the guise of hospitality to those who they deemed less fortunate?

He looked into her eyes. She had damn pretty eyes, he thought, feeling himself melt a little. For him, it was a brand-new sensation and he wasn't quite sure just what to do with it yet. Not without further examination.

"Because I'd like you to," he said softly.

For just the tiniest second, the way he looked at her made Denise's knees feel as if they were going to buckle like cardboard left out in the rain. The panic that caused made her grab handfuls of sarcasm and spread it liberally around—a magic circle to ward off men who could hurt her heart.

"And I should drop everything because you want me to do something?"

"Not everything." He placed his hand over the hammer she was holding, just in case she had any ideas. His foot was far too tempting a target for her to resist. "Just your attitude."

Just who did he think he was, coming in, criticizing everything about her? "And just what's wrong with my attitude?"

"Nothing," he allowed, his smile engaging. "If you happen to be a Viking about to sack a village. In that case, you'll be all prepared for anything that came your way. However, your attitude needs a little adjusting in light of these more modern, less violent times."

She knew it. He was laughing at her. "And you've elected yourself as chief adjuster." The question was almost a snarl.

Will fell back on his endless good humor, determined not to let her bait him this time. He was already having trouble recognizing himself. "I'd like the opportunity to do a little tweaking, yes."

There was no reason in the world for her pulse to jump that way over a word as stupid as "tweaking."

But there was no denying that her pulse was definitely jumping.

"Why?" she breathed.

Games were for people who knew how to play them. He wasn't even sure how to pick up the board pieces.

"Because I find myself very attracted to you, Denise Cavanaugh. Don't ask me why. Maybe I have a weakness for women who drive big-rigs with carousel horses stored in them, I don't know. All I know is that I'd like to see more of you. Preferably without having to worry about you biting off my head every two seconds." He gestured around the grounds. "Maybe you're a little softer, a little more at ease away from all this responsibility you're shouldering."

So, he wanted her softer, did he? Why? So he could pounce and not find a hard landing? She'd show him softer all right.

"What you see is what you get." She bit her lip, realizing that perhaps that didn't come out quite the way she wanted it to. "Figure of speech," she muttered disparagingly.

He grinned. Under the bravado, he had a hunch, was a very uncertain young woman. It would help him endure the attack.

"Understood."

Will saw her father approaching them again, a curious expression on his face. The man was probably wondering how he came to still be standing upright after ten minutes in the company of Denny, the man slayer. Will raised his voice, calling out to him.

"Mr. Cavanaugh, I'd like to invite you and your daughter and granddaughter for dinner at the Shady Lady."

Tate joined them. He welcomed the chance to get away from the makeshift kitchen and the meals that came out of it, even if he usually had a hand in making them.

"Is that a restaurant?" Tate hadn't noticed any establishment by that name on their way in, but there was a whole other side to this town he hadn't had a chance to see yet.

Will shook his head. "No, sir, that's the name of our ranch."

Tate rubbed his chest in small, concentric circles, a habit he had of late when he was thinking, Denise noted. She was quick to take advantage of the opportunity she hoped was opening up.

"We don't have to if you don't want to, Dad."

Oh, but he did want to. It would be good to get away for a while, and think of something other than the troubles surrounding them.

"A man never turns down an invitation for dinner, Denny. It's not polite." He looked at Will. "Just give us directions, Will. We'll be there."

"And I'll do better than that. I'll come by tonight to take you there myself."

If he drove, they'd be trapped there, Denise thought. "We can find our own way the—''

"That'll be very kind of you," Tate told Will, cutting Denise off.

Will nodded. "I'll be here at six," he promised. "But right now, I'm afraid I have to leave."

Tate nodded, too. "Thanks for all your help."

Will took his leave, feeling not unlike a man who had bid on a mystery box, not quite sure just what he was about to receive.

Denise went back to work even before Will was out of earshot. "You can go with Audra, Dad. I'm not going."

Tate sighed. If he lived forever, he wasn't going to figure her out. From where he'd stood, watching the two of them, he'd had the impression that there was something humming between them. Something good. He followed her back to the fun house.

"I'm the one who's supposed to get more ornery with age, Denny, not you." She merely made an unintelligible sound in response as she set the ladder back against the side of the building. Tate held it in place as she climbed up again. "What've you got against the boy?"

If Will Cutler were a boy, there'd be no problem. "He's a man, not a boy, Dad, and why are you so sold on him?" She bit back the flash of temper. Her father was far too willing to take people at face value.

Tate glanced over his shoulder. Will was just pulling out of the lot. He'd stayed on far longer than Tate had thought he would. And he did damn fine work.

"Because he seems like the decent sort and I think you could do with a little company outside the crew."

Hadn't her father learned anything after what she'd been through? Why wasn't he trying to protect her instead of encouraging her to become a walking target again? "I'm doing just fine."

"Are you, Denny?" He looked up concerned. "A woman your age—"

"Should be around people she cares about, doing what she wants to do." Her tone softened. He meant well. "And I am—on both counts."

Tate took the hammer from her as she climbed down again. "You need someone to take care of you, Denny. I can't do that anymore."

So that's what it was. Guilt. She did her best to absolve him of it. "That's a hopelessly old-fashioned idea, Dad. I can take care of myself and Audra, thank you very much."

It wasn't a matter of being incapable, it was a matter of need. "Everyone needs someone to lean on once in a while."

She smiled at him. He'd been both mother and father to her for more years than she had fingers and toes. "I have you."

The smile on his lips was rueful, tired. "I'm not much good anymore."

It broke her heart when he talked that way. She knew it was useless to try to talk him into going to see a doctor about the way he felt physically. But the least she could do was bully him into feeling better about himself.

"Now you listen to me, Tate Cavanaugh. You're just as good as you ever were and you've earned the right to slow down a little." Reaching up, she threaded her arm around his shoulder. "You've worked hard all your life, now let me take care of you."

A twinkle entered his eyes. "Does that mean indulging me a little?"

She knew where he was going with this. "You want me to go to this thing at the Cutlers's ranch tonight, don't you?"

"Yes."

She blew out a breath, surrendering. She never could say no to her father. "I suppose I can."

Tate caught her up in a hug. He had a feeling about that Cutler boy. A good feeling. Releasing Denise, he grinned at her. "That's my girl."

She wished she could have mustered the same kind of enthusiasm as he did, she thought darkly. But she had a very uneasy feeling that meeting Will Cutler on his home ground was not going to be good.

4

———◆———

"Will's bringing a woman?" Kent stared at his mother as Zoe Cutler set extra places at the table. Many extra places.

Finding a summons from his father to attend dinner on his answering machine when he walked into his house not half an hour ago, Kent had come more out of a sense of curiosity than anything else. Smack in the middle of the Cutler siblings, he felt himself to be the perfect balance between Will and Quint, his two more serious-minded brothers and Hank and Morgan, his younger, more flamboyant and fiery brother and sister.

Zoe spared her middle child a look that could only be described as barely harnessed joy laced with anticipation. "So he said."

Kent counted the extra places. There were five in all. One for him, one for Will. That left three unaccounted for. "How many women did Will say he was bringing?"

"Just one." Zoe moved a glass half an inch to

the right, then back again. She was admittedly nervous. Will had never brought a woman home before. "The other two places are for her family."

So it was a family affair, was it? This sounded way too serious for his oldest brother. "He's bringing them here?"

Kent looked around his parents' dining room, a room that Will had personally designed and remodeled. It was a given that when Will signed onto a project, he was there from inception to fruition. Kent tried to imagine the sort of woman who would capture his serious-minded brother's fancy and failed.

"Why here? Why not his own place?"

"Maybe he feels more comfortable bringing her here. He said he was bringing her father and her daughter, too."

"Daughter?" Kent echoed. This really sounded serious, he mused, still amazed. "Do you know the last time Will brought a female into the house?" He didn't wait for a response. "Fifteen years ago. It was Queenie."

Zoe thought of the stray collie her son had taken in. Queenie had long since gone to her reward. With deliberate movements, she refolded a napkin. "I am well aware of your older brother's interactions with women, Kent. Or lack thereof." She carefully replaced the silverware on the napkin. "Next to you, he was the one I despaired about the most."

Kent broke off a piece of a roll, his eyes widening. "Me?"

She fixed him with a look. "You." She glanced at her watch. Will should be arriving at any moment. Where on earth was Jake? "In the last five years, you spent more time with your horse, the cattle and the men than with any women."

The cause, more than anything, had been a romance that had turned sour on him. Kent's way of handling the hurt was to cut himself off from the possibility of repeating the error. He didn't believe in getting back into the saddle after being thrown when it came to the fairer sex.

"Thank goodness Brian Gainsborough had a daughter instead of a son," she said, mentioning the name of the man who had been her husband's best friend. "If she hadn't come out here on a magazine assignment, who knows if you'd have ever come around again?"

Kent frowned, not too pleased with the assessment he'd just received at his mother's hands. "You make me sound like a lost cause."

Humor curved her lips. "Well?"

Coming up behind her, Jake placed his arms around his wife's waist. Five children and Zoe still felt as trim as the young girl he'd first fallen in love with.

"He would have come around, Zoe. Watching us, he would have eventually realized how much he was missing by not being married." Jake stole a kiss to prove his point. "It would have gotten through to even his thick skull eventually." He laughed, releasing Zoe, then rubbed his hands together in anticipation of the meal as he eyed the set table. Only genetics kept him from having a weight problem. No one cooked like Zoe. His eyes swept along the place settings, doing a mental tally. Jake glanced at Kent. "So when is your lady coming back?"

His lady. It had a nice sound to it, Kent thought. And even a nicer feel. He missed Brianne more than he thought was possible. It amazed him how far removed he now was from the distant, brooding man he'd been when he'd first met her.

"As soon as she gets things settled in Connecticut and New York." It couldn't be soon enough for him.

Jake studied his son. "Maybe you and Hank can make it a double wedding."

A smile as enigmatic as his mother's played on his lips. "Maybe," Kent allowed.

"Why you old horse thief," Will declared, walking in on the tail end of the conversation. If Kent said maybe, he meant yes. "You never let things like that out unless you've already made up your mind to go through with it. God, Mom," Will greeted his mother with a bear hug, "you're losing two at once." He grinned. "Must feel great."

Kent turned around, a ready retort on his lips. One

look at the company Will had ushered in with him and Kent set aside his instruction on where Will could put his observation.

So this was the woman who'd managed to bring his brother to life. He had to give Will points for taste. She was a beauty. The woman was small and slender, but there was a look about her that said she could handle herself in any situation. She was nothing like what he figured Will would end up with. He'd always envisioned his brother with someone small and delicate, a woman who needed to be taken care of. Will had been a caretaker for as long as he could remember.

They looked like each other, Denise thought, her eyes shifting from one brother to the other. Tall, blond, good-looking, one more chiseled than the other. The word "cowboy" in big, bold letters sprang to mind. Will was taller and a little broader through the shoulder than his younger brother, but there was no mistaking the resemblance.

And they both looked like their father she realized after a beat. Denise tried to guess what Jacob Cutler had looked like as a younger man. Probably more like Will than the other one, she guessed. His eyes were kind. Like Will's.

It's thoughts like that are going to land you in a whole lot of trouble if you're not careful, Denny, she upbraided herself.

Will stepped back so that both his parents could

get a better view of their dinner guests. "Mom, Dad, I'd like you to meet Tate Cavanaugh, his daughter, Denise, and her daughter, Audra." Will inclined his head toward his family. "Tate, Denise, these are my parents, Zoe and Jake Cutler."

Kent cleared his throat, stepping forward. "Aren't you forgetting someone?"

Kent smiled more readily these days, Will noticed. That would be Brianne's handiwork. Will grinned at his brother.

"I try, little brother, I surely do try, but you just won't go away." He looked at the man and woman he'd driven over. "This is my brother, Kent. He's the one who never left home."

Jake intervened before his two sons decided to go at it, kidding or not. He thrust his wide hand toward Denise. "What he means is that Kent runs the ranch for us." He winked at Tate, one father to another. "After more than thirty years, I've decided to become a gentleman rancher and let someone else handle the headaches."

Zoe exchanged glances with Will. Only she knew just how hard turning over the reins had actually been for Jake. It had only happened at all because he'd suffered a heart attack. The doctor had ordered complete rest. Rather than let them sell the ranch, Kent had taken over running it. Kent had always been the one who loved the ranch the most, who saw himself as a rancher even as his brothers and sister sought careers in other directions. It seemed only natural that he be the one to take over.

Zoe shook their hands one at a time, smiling warmly. "Welcome to our home, Mr. Cavanaugh, Denise."

"Tate, please," Tate insisted, instantly feeling at home. You could always tell a lot, he judged, by the way a person welcomed you into their home. These were good people. Just the kind of parents he figured someone like Will would have.

"How about me? I'm down here, too," Audra piped up. She held her hand up in the air, offering it to the adults at large. She wanted someone to shake it, too.

The next minute, she squealed as Will picked her up in his arms.

"You sure are, Audra." He winked at her, making her giggle. "Didn't you know that people always save the best for last?"

"I'm the best?" Audra's eyes shone as she looked at the man she had already decided she was in love with.

Will pretended to look around the room. "Don't see anyone here who would argue that," he told her, then looked at Kent. "Do you?"

Kent shook his head. "Nope." He put his hands out to take Audra from his brother. "Come here and sit by me."

Watching her daughter brought a smile to Denise's lips. Audra was eating up the attention. For a second the little girl seemed to debate between the two men, then in true steadfast fashion, Audra made up her mind to remain with the man who had brought her. "I want to sit next to Will."

Kent nudged Will for Audra's benefit. "Seems to me you've got an admirer, brother."

Will grinned. He couldn't help glancing at Denise. "One out of two isn't bad."

If she wasn't careful, this man could easily slip under her guard. Squaring her shoulders, Denise sniffed. "She's too young to know better."

Suddenly realizing she might very well have insulted Will's mother, Denise quickly glanced in the woman's direction. Instead of a frown, she saw a very enigmatic smile on the woman's lips. Denise didn't know whether to be relieved or puzzled.

The one thing she knew was that she was welcomed. The Cutlers went out of their way to make them all feel right at home. Even so, Denise was astounded at the ease with which all the Cutlers, particularly Zoe and Jake, navigated the waters of neighborliness.

Before dinner and then throughout the meal, Zoe chatted with her as if they were old friends while Kent and Will took turns entertaining a very pleased-looking Audra. And it seemed to Denise that absolutely no time went by before her father and Jake were talking as if they'd spent their entire lives in close proximity.

Taking a breath, Denise mentally stepped back for a moment to absorb what was going on around her. Sometimes, when she grew restless, when their time on the road seemed endless and things were going badly, this was the kind of life she envisioned for the three of them. Sitting at a table, talking to friends, not having to worry about keeping on schedule, or about equipment that needed renovation. Or, in the early days, worrying about the weather robbing them of their income because it suddenly turned inclement and no one came to the carnival or to the fair.

Denise pressed her lips together. She'd always loved the smell of the open road, but this, she had to admit, was nice.

Very nice.

Stuffed to the proverbial gills, Tate sat back in his chair and sighed contentedly. He couldn't eat another bite, even though the strawberry shortcake Zoe had brought out—after the apple pie and homemade ice cream—was out of this world. He smiled at his hostess.

"I don't know when I've ever had better, Zoe. My ex-wife, bless her, couldn't cook up anything but mischief. She passed her talent down to Denny there." He saw the warning look in Denise's eyes. Denny, he knew, hated to be talked about, especially in front of strangers. But he didn't feel as if these people were strangers. Not from the first moment he met them. He grinned at her. "She's the greatest daughter in the whole world, but the only business she has in the kitchen is getting a glass of water."

Zoe had seen the look pass between father and daughter. She knew embarrassment when she saw it. "I'm sure she has a lot of other fine attributes."

"That she does," Tate quickly agreed. "She takes care of the whole crew, and I don't mind saying that she's the glue that keeps us all together."

Denise flushed, looking away. She wished her father wouldn't go on like this. She did what had to be done, nothing more. She'd been doing it for so long, she couldn't picture hanging back, not taking charge. It was who she was. Or who her family and friends needed her to be.

Will found himself thinking that he had never seen glue kept in such a tempting container. But right now, that glue looked as if she would rather be somewhere else. He was happy to oblige.

He moved his chair back. "Want to get some air?" he suggested. Then, leaning closer to her ear, he confided in a stage whisper. "If you don't leave the table now, my mother is just going to keep on putting out desserts in front of you and expecting you to eat them until you explode."

A smear of strawberry running along her cheek, Audra's eyes grew brighter still. "More dessert?"

There was no mistaking the hope in her voice. Desserts were a luxury that were few and far between when they were on the road. Her mother had a strict policy about the amount of sugar she could eat. Tonight was like a huge party to her.

"Audra, it's not polite to ask," Denise chided. The little girl was already too energetic. By the time they left here, Audra would be bouncing off any surface they found.

Zoe looked as if she had stepped into heaven. It had been a long time since she'd had a child to fuss over and she meant to enjoy herself.

"It's not only polite here," Zoe countered, "It's downright welcomed." Rising, she extended her hand to the little girl. "Come with me, Audra, you can have your pick."

"Uh-oh, get the stomach pump." Jake laughed. "Your granddaughter's going to feel as if she's died and gone to heaven," he assured Tate. If memory served, there were three other desserts left over in the refrigerator. "She definitely isn't going to know what to eat first."

Denise caught her lower lip between her teeth dubiously.

It didn't take much for Will to read the look in her eyes.

"It's okay," he assured her. "She's a mother first and a mad hostess second. My mother won't let Audra get sick."

Getting up, he looked at Denise expectantly. She made no move to join him. A smile quirked at the corners of his mouth.

"We don't have to go out," he whispered, his breath slipping sensually along her cheek, "if you're afraid to be alone with me."

Her chin shot up. She was on her feet in an instant. Will suppressed his smile. He knew that would get to her. Pleased, he extended his hand to Denise. She ignored it and went ahead of him to the door.

Covertly taking in the scene, Jake smiled at Tate as their children walked out. "I think we may have something going on here, Tate."

Tate rubbed his chest, trying to rub the ache away. It would go soon, just as it had all the other times. He'd eaten too much, that was all.

He'd seen the same spark, the same light passing between them that Jake had. Tate had his fingers crossed for all the reasons he'd given Denise. "I surely do hope so, Jake. I surely do hope so."

Walking onto the porch, Will closed the door behind them, shutting out the sounds from within. There were two rockers directly by the door, but he saw that she ignored them. Probably too domestic for her to sit on a porch and rock, he guessed.

The moonlight greeted Denise as if it were an old friend, its long, silvery fingers caressing her skin with reserved affection. It made her look so beautiful that Will could feel the ache in his gut, twisting there like a knife.

So this was how it felt to really want someone, he thought. He wasn't certain he actually liked the feeling. There was a frustration woven through it he wasn't sure how to handle.

Nerves danced through her, bringing every fiber in her to attention. She felt as if she was waiting...anticipating...

She didn't want to be.

Denise moved her shoulders restlessly, as if trying to shrug off the feeling. She shouldn't have come out here with him this way, even if part of her had wanted to.

Wanting to only made it worse.

Desperate, she looked for something to say, something to cut into the sultry silence that hung around them. She chose the obvious. And the inane. At least it was something.

"Dinner was wonderful."

She'd get no argument from him on that score. Will was proud of his mother's abilities. More than that, he was proud of his mother. Hell, he thought, he was proud of the whole lot of them.

"My mother could make a feast out of a picture of a chicken." A smile played on his lips as he remembered. "There were times when I was growing up that she almost had to."

The remark took Denise by surprise. She'd had

the impression that they had always lived here, on this vast, beautiful ranch, in this fine house. She regarded him closely, wondering if he was just making this up. "You were poor?"

There'd been times when they were certain they'd lose the ranch, lose everything. But each time, they managed to somehow pull together and pull through. That was what made the Shady Lady so precious to each of them—and what made him so proud of all of them.

"Only as far as money went," he told her. "We've always been rich in determination." Will leaned back against the railing, looking at her rather than the sprinkling of stars that were out. She shone more brightly than they did when she smiled. "We got that from both parents, just the way I imagine you got your determined streak from yours."

She shrugged indifferently. The plural term didn't apply. "The only thing my mother was ever determined about was leaving the carnival and my father. Which she did. As quickly as she could." Without realizing it, she ran her hands along her arms, as if to ward off the feeling of being dismissed by a parent who has never lived up to the full responsibility the word required. "I was five years old at the time."

He moved closer to her, slipping his arm around her shoulders. "I'm sorry. Must have been rough on you."

She began to shrug him off, then didn't. She let herself absorb the sensation, if only for a moment. "We managed."

But not without scars, he thought. "Is that why you're so tough-skinned? Because your mother hurt you so badly when she left?"

Denise took offense at the label. "My mother didn't hurt me—badly or otherwise—when she left. I couldn't have cared less. We never got along, even then." Her eyes narrowed as she looked up at him. "And I am not tough-skinned," she insisted. "I'm sensible, remember?"

Will inclined his head, far more intent on watching the way the moonlight shimmered on her lips than on winning any point of contention between them. "If you say so."

Denise was standing toe-to-toe with him, her chin raised. Her mouth less than six inches from his. "I say so."

The angle made the target far too tempting to resist. He would have been more than human if he could have and Will had always said that he was only a mere mortal man. And mortal men had their limits.

Will was face-to-face with his.

Without consciously being aware of doing it, Will threaded his fingers through her hair, cupping the back of her head. Ever so slowly, he tilted it back even more, bringing his lips closer to hers. He thought he could detect the erratic beating of her heart, but that could have just been his imagination.

Or maybe the sound of his own heart.

"How sensible?" The question whispered along the outline of her mouth.

The words felt as if they were all sticking inside her throat. "Very."

"Oh?"

Denise thought she nodded, but she wasn't sure. She couldn't seem to tear her eyes away from his. Couldn't move from the spot even though she knew she should.

"Too sensible to let you kiss me."

The smile was in his eyes instead of on his lips. "Mind if I put that theory to the test?"

Before she could answer, he brought his mouth down to hers.

Will felt his pulse quicken immediately on contact. Kissing her was everything he'd thought it would be. And maybe a little more.

She tasted not of the strawberries that his mother had laced all over her cake, but of something far more exotic, far more stirring. Trying to place the flavor, he deepened the kiss.

Within seconds, the quest to label the elusive taste was abandoned. A second more and he couldn't even remember wanting to know.

Or his own name, for that matter.

What throbbed foremost in his mind was that he'd been waiting all his life to feel this way.

Disoriented and wild about the feeling.

He pulled her closer to him, sampling more, wanting more.

Wanting her.

Denise's head swam, spinning almost out of control, like the center of the whirling dervish ride that Audra loved so much. Her arms around his neck, she clung to Will for support and because it felt so good to feel his body against hers.

The sensation began to set off alarms. The last time she'd felt this way, she'd had a baby to show for it nine months later. A baby and a broken heart.

History was *not* going to repeat itself.

With a strangled cry, she pulled her head back. "No," she cried hoarsely. "No."

5

Feeling every inch an intruder, Kent cleared his throat loudly, warning his brother and the woman Will was holding that they were not alone.

Talk about rotten timing, Kent thought disparagingly.

Startled, Will and Denise jumped apart like two people on the wrong end of a cattle prod.

Kent shifted uncomfortably in the doorway when they looked in his direction. "Look, I wouldn't for the world bother you right now, but I think you two better come inside." He nodded toward the house behind him.

The moment and the shock of realizing that she was every bit as vulnerable as she'd once been, that every precaution she'd so painstakingly put into place was now lying shredded on the ground, null and void, were instantly shoved to the background. The somber look on Kent's face drove a sharp stake of fear straight through Denise's heart.

It didn't do much less for Will. More stoic than

emotional, Kent wasn't the type to dramatize anything. Or to just wander in where he undoubtedly knew he wasn't wanted. Will raised a silent, questioning brow as he looked at his brother.

Kent wasn't elaborating, Denise thought. Panic frayed nerves that had already been undone by Will. "What's the matter?" She hurried past Kent into the house even as she asked. "Is it Audra?"

"No, it's your father." Kent shut the door behind him.

She looked at Kent incredulously. She felt her heart being squeezed. "Dad?"

Denise immediately thought the worst. It had become her nature to gravitate to that rather than hold onto hopeful possibilities. She looked around, struggling with guilt, half expecting to see her father lying slumped on the floor. She shouldn't have listened to him. She shouldn't have brought him here. All that rich food—what had she been thinking?

Guilt grew larger. What she'd been thinking was that she wanted a respite and had used her father's urging as an excuse, that's what.

And now her father was paying for it.

Audra ran in from the other room. Her face was bewildered as she wrapped her arms around her mother and pulled her into the living room. "Mama, Mama, Grampa's sick."

Tate Cavanaugh was lying on the sofa, his long, lanky frame filling it from one end to the other. His head was down while his feet were elevated, propped up by a number of pillows. By the expression on his face, he felt foolish, as if he'd involuntarily made a spectacle of himself.

"I'm all right." It pricked his conscience that Denise turned completely pale when she walked into the room and saw him lying like this. "I got a little dizzy. It's just indigestion, nothing else." He tried to turn his head to look at his hostess and found that he didn't have enough strength to complete the maneuver. "No reflection on your cooking, Zoe."

"My cooking be hanged," she retorted. "It's not anything as simple as indigestion and you know it, Tate Cavanaugh." She fixed him with the same intent look she'd used on her children when they were growing up to extract the truth from them. "When's the last time you had a complete physical?"

Tate shrugged, staring at the ceiling. "Can't say as I remember."

She knew it, Denise thought. She knew she should have bullied him into going to see a doctor six months ago, when he'd first started looking so drained. Denise bit back self-disgust and mounting panic.

"That's because the last time he had a complete physical, the doctor held him upside down by his ankles and slapped him on the rump." She looked at her father accusingly. "He hasn't had one since the day he was born."

Tate knew it was useless to argue with the truth. He didn't even try.

"Men," Zoe muttered, tucking another pillow under Tate's legs. "Stubborn jackasses, every one of them and I'm in a position to know." She shot a look toward her husband for good measure, in case he'd forgotten how much grief he'd given her when the same set of circumstances had embraced him.

Denise noted that there was no hesitation on Zoe's part. Having taken charge of the situation, she was behaving as if she'd encountered all this before. Keeping her own hands on Audra's shoulders in silent comfort, Denise longed to have someone reassure her. Maybe it was selfish of her, but she wanted someone to still the mounting fear she felt.

She was ashamed of herself for even fleetingly indulging in self-pity when her father needed her.

"What do you think is wrong?" Denise asked.

Zoe stepped back, her words stern, her smile silently encouraging both father and daughter. "Besides an overdose of stubbornness, I'd say your father might be on the verge of having a heart attack." Her smile faded into concern. "If he hasn't already had one."

"Nonsense, I'm fine." To prove it, Tate tried to sit up. It wasn't nearly as easy as it should have been. "I'd know if I were having a heart attack or not."

"Not necessarily." Jake placed a wide hand on

the man's thin chest and gently restrained him. "You don't have to drop in your tracks to have a heart attack, Tate. Those little ones can really do a number on you without you knowing it. Sometimes, they just scamper right over you, taking away a piece at a time." Empathy rose in his eyes. "You look just the way I did just before I had mine." Even though five years had since passed, right now it felt like yesterday. "When I got to the hospital, the doctor surprised me by saying that I'd already had a swarm of little attacks." He knew how important it felt to cling to the lie. Knew, too, what that could ultimately do to a man. "I thought it was indigestion, too."

That was all she had to hear. "You're going to see a doctor," Denise declared.

Jake nodded. "That'd be your best bet," he agreed, looking at Tate.

A cold and clammy feeling slid over Denise's heart, taking it hostage. She had an awful feeling that they were fighting against the clock. Denise turned toward Jake. He'd come through this, and he looked just fine now. No longer an optimist, she still held onto that comforting thought. "Where's the nearest hospital?"

"Oh, we don't have to go tonight," her father protested.

She knew he hated being fussed over. Too bad. "Tonight." The word sounded very nearly like an order. For good measure, she added, "Now." Denise was afraid she'd already allowed too much time to lapse.

"There's one in Serendipity," Will told her. When she looked at him, his heart twisted in his chest. He doubted very much that she knew she looked like a frightened little girl. He wanted to take her into his arms, to comfort her, but there was no time for that. "I'll take you there," he added softly.

Denise would have rather just taken her father herself. This was a family matter. But with no transportation of her own, she was in no position to turn Will down.

Biting her lower lip, she looked at Audra, hesitating. Audra shouldn't have to be put through this.

Zoe was one step ahead of her.

"We'll take care of Audra," she promised.

But Audra suddenly looked uncertain about the state of affairs. "Mama?" Her eyes darted nervously toward her grandfather.

One look at the wide blue eyes and Will could feel the questions piling up in the child's head. Kneeling down to her level, he picked her up in his arms. "Your grandfather's going to be just fine, honey," Will solemnly told Audra.

She placed her small hands on either side of his face, as if she could feel if he was lying to her. "You promise?"

"I promise." There was nothing but conviction

in his voice. Will knew this wasn't a time to hedge his bets and remain on the safe side the way he was wont to do. Audra needed a promise to hold on to, to comfort her. He glanced toward his brother. "Kent?"

"Way ahead of you, as usual, brother." Grinning at Audra, he took the little girl from Will.

Will turned his attention to Tate. "Can you walk?" he asked kindly.

The question rattled Tate's frail hold on his dignity. "Of course I can walk." He sat up in one movement. After a split-second delay, the room began to swim before him. He swayed, and grabbed the arm of the sofa.

Denise bit back a cry. Her father had turned completely white. She was at his side, determined to give him whatever support he needed to manage his exit despite her diminutive size.

"Lean on me," she urged.

"Been doing that for too long as it is," Tate murmured, but he offered no resistance when she took his arm and slung it over her shoulders.

The woman didn't have the sense she was supposed to have been born with, Will thought. Annoyed at her heroics, he was at Tate's other side immediately, helping the man to his feet and bearing up to most of the weight.

"You're going to strain something," Will told her sharply.

Denise bristled at the chastising. Was he going to tell her what to do even now?

"It's my 'something' to strain and my father," she snapped back.

Even in his present weakened state, Tate could feel the heat traveling between them. Refereeing, he tried to muster a smile.

"Why don't the two of you just get me to that doctor before I regain my strength and change my mind?"

Denise glared at Will. What was it about this man that brought out the worst in her? The look she flashed her father was contrite.

"Sorry, Dad," she murmured. Nothing was more important than getting her father to the doctor. She couldn't let anything else distract her. Not even Will.

Tate sighed. Even that hurt. "Not nearly as sorry as I am."

She looked pale and wan, Will thought, glancing toward Denise as he drove them home from the hospital. It had been a long night. It was late now, and the countryside had retreated into the inside of an inkwell.

Her eyes closed, Denise was leaning her head back against the seat. He could easily guess what was going on in her mind right now. He'd been there himself not all that many years ago. Thinking about it only made the situation worse.

"He'll be all right, Denny."

Denny.

Her eyes moistened instantly at the sound of the nickname. She wanted to cry out and tell him that he had no right to call her that. That only her father could call her that.

But the words never came out. Too many other words, too many other emotions got in the way. She felt so horribly confused. And so very afraid.

Denise pressed her lips together. She couldn't keep lashing out at Will. He was just trying to be helpful. And yet, when she opened her mouth, the words that seemed to find their way out were antagonistic. It was as if, if she didn't cling to her anger, she would fall completely apart.

"How do you know that?" she demanded of him. "What if—"

He knew where she was going with that. To a very dark, hollow place.

"Don't do that to yourself," he warned. "'What ifs' don't necessarily happen and there's no use torturing yourself over them. Just wasted effort all around." He could see by the set of her jaw that he wasn't getting through. He continued at it doggedly. "Doc Black's a good cardiologist. He treated my father. Back then, he was at St. Augustine's in Butte."

It had been a hell of a drive there that night, Will thought. Quint driving the van as if it were a sports car and the very wind was under its wheels, he and Kent in the back, holding on to their father between them. And their mother talking to Jake all the while as if this was just another Sunday drive. Morgan had met them at the hospital, as pale as Denise was now. Things like that shook you down to your very roots, made you aware of what was important in life and what wasn't.

He'd almost forgotten that lesson, he realized. Until today.

"He was one of the first doctors to sign on when Serendipity Memorial opened," Will told her, wondering if she was hearing any of this. He was desperately trying to keep her mind occupied.

She nodded absently. "It looks new. The hospital," she tagged on as an afterthought.

"That's because it is." The quarter moon hung above them in a perfect crescent, guiding him home. "It opened its doors June 1, 1996."

Denise sat up and looked at him. "You know the exact date?"

He grinned. He knew the exact date of all the buildings he'd had a hand in designing. Until he had one of flesh and blood, the buildings were like his children. "I should. I designed it."

Denise should have realized that by the way he

knew his way around so well. She'd just assumed it was because he'd brought his father there.

"Nice work," she murmured. She shifted in her seat, feeling as if every bone in her body ached. No matter what she did, she just couldn't get comfortable tonight. Not after leaving her father in that room, even though she knew it was the only right thing to do.

"Thanks, I try." Will read her restlessness correctly. "Denny, there are worse things to face than an angioplasty." His own father had had to have bypass surgery. Out of the corner of his eye, Will saw her frown. "As a matter of fact, your father's a lucky man."

He was lying in a strange bed in a strange hospital, waiting for a man whom he didn't know to make a hole in his thigh and snake a tube up into the chambers of his heart in the morning. And all of it was going to cost a fortune. A fortune they didn't have. She hardly saw that as being lucky.

"How do you figure that?"

She had to ask? Will thought. "He was diagnosed in time. In a couple of weeks, he'll be like a new man." He looked at her. "Really."

She merely nodded her head. Will was probably right. She really, really wished that she could believe in something again. That she could believe that every cloud in the sky had a silver lining and didn't just represent another thunderstorm.

Her mouth quirked. "I kind of like the old one."

The woman could probably find something to argue about in everything she came across. "Then he'll be that, except better." Will paused, knowing that she was probably going to hand his head to him for pushing. He pushed anyway. "Denise, what else is wrong?"

She tried to look nonchalant as she slanted a glance at him. "Else?"

She didn't do innocent very well, but maybe that was to her credit. Lying was never an admirable attribute. "There's something else eating away at you. What is it?"

"There's nothing else eating away at me," she snapped, then instantly felt guilty. She looked down at her hands rather than at his face. "I don't know how I'm going to pay for this."

So that was it. Part of Will had thought that perhaps it had something to do with what happened between them earlier. Heaven knew, it was still on his mind. On his mind and weaving itself into a knot in the pit of his stomach. A knot he wasn't sure what he was going to do about.

But they were discussing her problem, not his.

"No insurance?"

Denise shook her head. It was always something she meant to look into, but had just never gotten around to it. There had never been any money left over to splurge on that. So she'd kept on playing the odds, hoping to win each hand.

"No nothing. Not even a nest egg to fall back on." Denise laughed shortly. It was either that, or bury her head in her hands, and she wasn't about to do that in front of anyone, least of all a man who had kissed her with a mouth hot enough to set off a forest fire. "All the eggs fell out of the nest a long time ago." She sighed, trying to rally. "I'll come up with something."

It sounded to Will as if she had a great deal of practice being creative. Eventually that had to get really difficult. "You always do?"

"Yeah, I always do." Denise glanced in his direction and saw the smile on his lips. Was he laughing at her? "What?"

"I was just thinking of your father." The road ahead of them forked. He took the right branch. "I thought, weak as he was, that he was going to have to be tied down to his bed when Doc Black said he had to stay in the hospital overnight and that he had to have surgery tomorrow."

She laughed softly to herself, picturing him. "He's a feisty soul when he has to be."

His eyes touched her lightly. A sliver of moonlight had made itself comfortable inside the car, caressing her face. "Must run in the family."

"Yes, it does," she said proudly. The ranch house was taking shape in the distance. "Well, there it is."

She felt a twinge of guilt. "We'll be getting out of your hair soon. I'm sorry you have to drive all the way back to town."

The outskirts of town was where he lived, so driving back was no inconvenience to him. But he wasn't thinking of his home now. He was thinking of her. "I don't have to drive all the way back to town."

"What do you mean?" She wasn't following him.

He glanced at the clock on the dashboard. It was close to midnight. "It's late. Why don't you and Audra stay at the ranch for the night? Longer if you like. My folks have got plenty of rooms. I ought to know, I helped add them on."

She knew how to put together and dismantle the rides with her eyes shut, but to be responsible for erecting a permanent structure, now that was something to be proud of.

Though she believed that the less she knew about Will, the better it was for her, curiosity got the better of her. "How long have you been at this?"

He didn't even have to think. "Ever since I built my first fort at the age of six. I can't remember a time when I wasn't sketching plans and then trying to make them a reality."

Denise could hear the pride in his voice. "It must be nice, having a gift like that."

He brought the car to a stop before the house.

"Everyone's got a gift, sometimes it just takes a while to find it."

She shook her head with a tinge of disgust. "I swear, you sound just like a greeting card."

If she thought to insult him, she missed her mark. "Nothing wrong with greeting cards."

"No," she agreed, "but they don't have very much to do with reality."

A smile played along his mouth. "Oh, I don't know, I always thought they brought out the best part of reality."

Denise shrugged, too tired to argue. "So, how do I get to town?"

He didn't quite follow her. "You mean in the morning?"

She got out of the car, closing the door in her wake. "No, I mean now—if you won't drive me."

She made it sound as if he was doing it solely to annoy her. "It's not a matter of 'won't,' but I think since Audra's probably already asleep that it's just a good idea for you to stay here. I'll take you into town in the morning."

"Don't you have to go to work?" He didn't have time to play chauffeur.

"It's all located in the same general area," he answered patiently, "Work, carnival grounds, hospital. No extra driving. We'll just get an early start in the morning."

Why was he making things more difficult for her? "Not if I get back tonight."

Will blew out a breath. "Do you argue about everything?"

Oh, so now this was her fault? Denise thought. No way. "I wouldn't have to argue if you agreed with me."

He had to laugh at her logic. "That's rich."

She fisted her hands at her waist. "No, that's right."

The woman was one of a kind. No one else Will knew ever made him lose his temper. "You know, until I met you, I thought my sister, Morgan, was the most headstrong female God ever created. But you've got her beat by a country mile."

She sniffed. "I'll take that as a compliment."

Why didn't that surprise him? "You would." He looked at her closely. "What are you afraid of?"

There went that male ego of his again, Denise thought. He probably thought it all had to do with him, with being afraid that she was growing much too vulnerable around him. Well, he was wrong.

"I'm not afraid of anything. I just don't like being in debt."

That was easily solved. "Then give us extra tickets." But he didn't really believe that was the whole reason. "Seems to me, Denny, that your life would be a whole lot more pleasant if you were."

She took offense instantly. "What?"

He had no intention of smoothing that over. "You heard me. You'd have a better time of it if you just learned to relax a little and accept a hand offered in friendship when it's extended."

"Is that what you're doing?" As if she didn't know better. Friends didn't kiss like that, didn't set out to numb your body and crack your soul.

"Yes."

Her eyes narrowed as she caught him in the lie. "And that kiss on the porch, was that friendship, too?"

"Yes." He refused to back down. "Just a special kind of friendship, that's all." He smiled, softening. Maybe she'd learn by example if he kept showing her. "Now can I tell my mother to make up an extra bed, or am I going to have to listen to her lecture me on my lack of manners because I couldn't convince you to stay?"

She wavered. If she were being honest, she really didn't relish the thought of being alone tonight. Her mind was far too active right now. And the scenarios it was going through were dreadful.

"Well, as long as I'd be doing you a favor...if you're sure your mother won't mind."

He smiled, triumphant but trying to be a good sport about it. "I'm sure. My mother would only mind if you and Audra went back to town tonight." For good measure, he reinforced his statement. "As a matter of fact, both my parents would."

Denise gave in. "All right, I suppose it wouldn't do any harm to stay the night."

It was an odd choice of words, Will thought, opening the front door. He couldn't begin to understand why she'd think it might harm anything if she and Audra spent the night, or even the next few nights at the Shady Lady. Getting this woman to accept an act of kindness was like pulling teeth. Very pretty teeth he conceded, but teeth nonetheless.

6

←————

Some of her wariness dropped off the moment Denise entered the living room and saw her daughter sleeping on the sofa. The crocheted throw that had graced the back of the black leathered upholstery was now lightly draped over the little girl. The night was cool, despite the season.

For a moment Denise paused, letting the sight get to her. Soothe her.

Audra looked so untroubled, so peaceful, she thought. A half smile curved her mouth. Wouldn't it be wonderful if she could somehow manage to keep things just that way for her daughter?

But that was just a pipe dream at best, and she didn't believe in those any longer. She knew they didn't have a prayer of coming true.

Jake and Zoe were on either side of her before Denise had taken five steps into the room.

"What did the doctor say?" Jake wanted to know.

Denise opened her mouth, but it was Will who

answered the question for her. "Mr. Cavanaugh has to stay at the hospital. The treadmill test they had him take showed a blocked artery. Doc Black wants to do an angioplasty on him in the morning."

Zoe pressed her lips together, taking in a deep breath as she relived her own ordeal and uncertainty. "That's what he said would have helped you, if you'd only gone in when you should have instead of waiting."

Jake nodded, his attention devoted to Denise. He took her hand in his and noted that it was icy. Why wasn't his son doing something about this state of affairs?

"Your daddy couldn't be in better hands, honey," he assured her. "Trust me."

There wasn't a single reason for her to believe anything this man, or any of them, were saying to her. She hadn't known any of them yesterday.

And yet...

And yet she did, Denise realized. She did trust them. And there was something infinitely comforting in being able to feel that trust. Rolling it over in her mind, she examined it from all angles, as if it were an exotic seashell she'd found in her path on the beach.

It was a strange feeling, trusting someone. One she wasn't accustomed to.

Taking charge again, Zoe slipped her arm around Denise's shoulders.

"So you'll be staying here?" Denise knew it was a rhetorical question. From the sound of her voice, Zoe had apparently made up her mind that she was having two extra people under her roof tonight. All she wanted from Denise was to have her rubber-stamp it.

Will grinned at his mother over Denise's head. "I talked her into it."

Did this man think that she was so swaddled in grief and concern that she'd lost the ability to speak? Why was he constantly answering for her? Denise set her mouth hard as she turned her eyes accusingly on him.

"And talked and talked."

The clanging noise in his head was the sound of two swords, crossing. The unofficial truce hadn't lasted long, Will thought. "Now what did I do wrong?"

She squared her shoulders, reacting to his tone. "I'm perfectly capable of answering your parents' questions on my own, thank you."

He wasn't about to get into another loud discussion with her in front of his parents. For the sake of harmony, he raised his hands in mock surrender.

"Sorry."

"Mama."

Audra was stumbling toward her, rubbing her eyes and dragging the throw that was now wrapped around her legs with her. Getting down on her knees, Denise immediately untangled her.

"Now look what you did," she tossed accusingly over her shoulder. "You woke her up. There, baby, it's okay."

Will could taste his temper rising. This woman really did bring out the worst in him, he thought grudgingly. "I wasn't the one who raised my voice."

Denise flushed. Rising, she dropped the throw on the sofa, then picked up a sleepy Audra. "Sorry, this is no way to repay your hospitality." The apology was directed more toward his parents than toward Will. "I'm just edgy."

Zoe slipped her arm around Denise's shoulders again, smiling at Audra in the bargain. "And you've got every reason in the world to feel that way. Your daddy's in the hospital, facing surgery and you're nervous for him. It's all perfectly natural."

Audra jerked her head up off her mother's shoulder. Her eyes were huge as she looked around the room, searching for her grandfather. "Grampa's in the hospital?"

Because it helped both of them cope, Denise stroked her daughter's head, gently pressing it back down against her shoulder.

"Shh, it's okay, baby. They're going to make Grampa all better. Fix him up just like that." She snapped her fingers for effect.

Audra solemnly nodded her head. "I know that."

She wished she had just a piece of that faith she saw now in her daughter's eyes. "Oh, and just how do you know that?"

Audra pointed a small index finger at Will. "Because Will promised."

He had no right to do that, Denise thought angrily. He had no right to get Audra to believe so strongly. What if something went wrong with the operation tomorrow? What could she possibly say to her daughter that would alleviate not only her grief at losing her beloved grandfather, but take away the pain of realizing that she'd been deceived by someone she believed in?

Denise's eyes narrowed as she turned to look at the offender. "Yes, he did, didn't he?"

Will didn't think he liked the tone of that, and he knew he didn't like the look in her eyes. But there wasn't anything he could say without getting into a row with her and now wasn't the best time. So he kept his peace and said nothing.

"Why don't I show you where you'll be staying?" Zoe suggested tactfully.

Audra let loose with an exaggerated version of a yawn. "Can Will carry me?"

Denise looked at her daughter in surprise. "But I'm already carrying you."

"I know, but Will's arms are more muscley and comfy." She smiled beguilingly at her hero.

Denise hesitated. She didn't want Audra getting attached to this man. And she definitely didn't want to do anything to encourage that attachment. They'd be gone in a matter of two weeks if the surgery was as unobtrusive as the doctor had made it sound. The last thing she wanted was for Audra to feel as if she'd left something behind when they went.

"Glad you noticed," Will said to Audra. "And I'd certainly love to carry you to your room." Will extended his arms to Audra. "That is, if your mother doesn't have any objections."

She had lots of objections, Denise thought vehemently. None, however, that she could voice right now, in front of witnesses who had bent over backward for her. Feeling as if she was on the spot, Denise had no choice but to surrender her daughter to Will.

Audra curled up like a contented kitten in his arms. "Okay, we can go now," she all but purred.

Denise rolled her eyes as she followed behind Zoe. She could hear Jake chuckling to himself in the background. Though she found nothing funny in the situation, she had to admit that the laugh had a comforting sound to it.

Just like the people and the house.

"Well, that didn't take very long," Will commented as he eased the guest door shut behind him.

Had he been a betting man, he would have laid

odds that Audra would stay awake for hours. But she'd dropped off to sleep five minutes into the story she begged him to tell her. The excitement had gotten the better of her.

Exhausted and keyed up at the same time, Denise dragged her hand through the back of her hair, letting it fall again.

"It took her a lot less time to fall asleep than it's going to take me." She seriously doubted that she was going to sleep a wink tonight. She looked at him, mildly curious. "Where did you get that story, anyway? Something your mother read to you?"

An amused glimmer entered his eyes. "No, it was actually kind of autobiographical."

She looked at him. With nowhere to go, she'd found herself listening to the whimsical tale of a boy, a boxful of freshly hatched wolf spiders and an inspired hunt for a wild pony in the canyon. And charmed by it.

"That mischievous little boy in the story was you?"

"Yes." He took her arm as naturally as if they'd always walked side by side. He sensed her tension. "Want to go outside for some air?"

"Sure." And then she shook her head as she slanted a look at Will's face. "I just can't picture you as being mischievous."

Wisps of other memories, long dimmed by time, floated through his mind. He held the front door open for her. "I was, until I realized that my parents needed help with the ranch and with my brothers and sister. Nothing like responsibility to drain the mischief right out of you."

But even as he said it, a fond smile played on his lips. If he resented any part of his youth, it wasn't evident, Denise thought.

Shouldering responsibility at too young an age. She could really relate to that. "Tell me about it."

Will turned, leaning his back against the railing. Looking at her. "I'd rather you told me about it."

She shrugged self-consciously. She shouldn't have said anything, she berated herself. Folding her hands before her, Denise looked off into the darkness straight ahead of her.

She could feel his eyes on her. "Nothing nearly as colorful as disobeying my parents—my father," she amended "and finding my own wild pony in the hills." She shrugged again, wishing she could shrug away his gaze as well. Or at least her reaction to it. "It's just something that slowly happened, that's all."

She said it as if the weight of that responsibility was making her bow submissively. It didn't fit in with what he was learning about her. "It wouldn't have happened if you didn't want it to."

She straightened. The next moment he saw the by-now-familiar lift of her chin.

"I take it you're speaking from experience?" she asked coolly.

He inclined his head. He knew when to go with responsibility and where and when to silently draw the line. "Yeah."

She wanted to take umbrage, but there was almost something genial in his response, so she let it ride. For now.

"I suppose I did want it." Ambivalent feelings ricocheted right and left like a handball with nowhere to land. "Maybe I even flattered myself that I could do a damn good job of it."

"And could you? Do you?" He figured he already had the answer to that, but it might do her some good to hear herself say it out loud.

Denise's eyes narrowed at what she perceived was a challenge. If she'd momentarily let the situation get the best of her, it was gone now. Her spirit was back and intact.

"Yes, I could and I do." She thought of the most recent turn of events, Harry quitting the crew. "Of course, with members of the crew dropping out on me, I don't know how much longer I can keep all this going."

A rueful smile slipped along her lips, tempting Will to kiss her. He didn't think she'd appreciate it right now. Probably take it to mean that he was belittling her problems in some fashion. So he worked at ignoring the very real, very urgent pull he felt.

He wasn't quite sure if he was rooting for victory or defeat in this case.

Denise stared up at the sky, idly wondering who else was gazing up at it at this very moment and how much more orderly their lives were than hers.

"Nobody runs away to the circus anymore and they certainly don't run away to work for someone who provides the rides for a carnival." She shoved her hands into her pockets. "I keep hiring people to replace the ones who've left, but they never last very long." Right now, they were the most shorthanded they'd ever been.

"Their itchy feet take them in other directions?" he guessed. Moonlight was gliding along her skin, the way he longed to.

"Something like that." Without thinking, she rotated her shoulders and stretched. There were tight kinks running the length of her back and the breadth of her shoulders. She felt as if she were a recent refugee from the rack.

The next moment, she felt Will's hands on her shoulders. Denise jumped, but managed to bite back the squeal of surprise.

"Easy." The tone Will used was the same one he'd once used on the pony he'd eventually won over and tamed. "I'm just trying to help you work out these knots." He gave a short laugh more from wonder than amusement. "I've come across boulders that were less tense."

She shifted self-consciously. He already knew more about her than she wanted him to. "How many boulders have you massaged?"

If his goal was to help her relax, he wasn't going to achieve it, Denise thought. There was absolutely no way she could relax around him, not when his hands were sending shock waves through her system like this.

"None," he said cheerfully. "Until now."

"Well, don't waste your time." Denise tried to turn away, but found that she wasn't going anywhere. He wouldn't let her. Instead he continued methodically working on her shoulders. Despite herself, Denise could feel some of the knots loosening. And it felt wonderful.

"I'll decide if my time's being wasted or not," he informed her mildly. "Just stay put. Maybe you'd rather sit down."

She didn't trust her knees to work again once she sat down. "Standing is fine."

What wasn't fine was what was happening. Will was turning her into liquid, she realized in alarm. Pure liquid.

Heated liquid.

Self-preservation kicked in. This time when she shrugged Will off, she stepped away from him as well. For safety's sake, she fortified herself with a deep breath before saying anything.

"I think that's enough."

Will grinned. If he didn't miss his guess, the lady was as affected by his touching her as he was. "If you say so."

"I say so," she reiterated emphatically. Not that it wasn't pleasurable, but she knew the danger in letting herself absorb that kind of pleasure. And where it would lead.

He looked toward the house. It was late. "Want to turn in?"

Denise shook her head, not wanting to be confined just yet. She knew she'd probably only spend the night tossing and turning. And worrying. "I won't be able to sleep."

"All right, care to go for a walk?"

The suggestion struck her as odd. Denise was accustomed to parking her trailer on the outskirts of a town or a city. There was usually at least one place to go. Here there was nothing but land and sky.

"Where's there to walk?"

He grinned, putting out his hand to her. "Everywhere."

She hesitated, then after a beat, she placed her hand in his.

And fervently hoped she wouldn't regret it.

Will took her to the clearing that was just behind what Morgan liked to refer to as the backyard. When he was a lot younger, he used to enjoy coming out here to think and clear his mind.

With no external distractions to capture her attention, Denise found the darkness that wrapped around her soothing. When she sighed, it felt as if she'd been holding her breath all evening.

"Seems to me that you've shouldered a great deal."

There were times she felt as if it was too much, but she always managed. Giving up was the alternative and she hated quitters.

"I can handle it. I have so far." And she prayed that Time wouldn't prove her a liar.

She had a young daughter to raise, an ailing father to care for and a business to run single-handedly, Will mentally listed. He knew people who would be overwhelmed by less. "Maybe you could take on a partner."

Denise laughed softly. "No one in his right mind would buy into the business."

Not that she could do anything by committee. She didn't have the patience for that. As long as she could remember, she'd always just forged ahead and done things. And her father had let her.

"The market for the independent provider is shrinking at a breathtaking speed." She set her mouth hard as she thought of the last dealing she'd had with the head of Zenith Rides. "There are organizations that do this sort of thing now, lease rides to country fairs and carnivals. I have to hustle for every contract, every deal." She couldn't help the bitter edge in her voice. There were times she did feel bitter. "It doesn't matter that we've always provided the rides. Someone comes along with a lower price, a better deal—" she shrugged helplessly "—they have us beat."

She glanced toward him and saw that he actually looked interested. Denise knew she was talking too much, but right now, it seemed to help steady her nerves.

"And then there's the cost of maintaining these rides, making sure they're safe. An organization can readily afford any problem it might run into, say, replacing a ride, putting out for an expensive repair. I can't." She shook her head, thinking of what the last premium had cost her. "An organization doesn't blink at the insurance costs that are involved. I not only blink, I shudder."

"So, what's the alternative?"

The question rubbed on a sore spot. "I don't have one." At least, not one she wanted to think about. "So I just go on."

She struck him as far too intelligent not to be taking all contingencies into consideration. "You've got to have an alternate plan."

"No, I don't," she insisted. Who was he to butt in, anyway? This was her problem, her life, not his. Why was he making noises as if he cared? If she started believing that, once he was out of her life, she'd have a hard time coping. "That way, I don't waste any necessary time or energy on it." She read his expression and could guess what he thought of her philosophy. "Maybe that's narrow of me, but like I said, we get by."

She deserved to do more than just get by. "How about your father's operation?"

Annoyance burrowed out a little further. "You let me worry about that."

The woman was incredible. "You're determined to bite every hand that's held out to you in friendship, aren't you?"

He was smiling at her, but he was judging her, nonetheless, Denise thought, and she didn't like it. Not one bit.

"Never knew an open hand yet that wasn't ready to close around something, take something from you when you weren't looking."

He stopped walking and looked at her. "And what do you think I'll take from you?"

"Nothing, because you won't get the chance." Her eyes dared him to even try.

Will studied her face for a long moment. "He hurt you that much?"

Denise tossed her head, pretending indifference. "Who?"

The hour was late and he didn't want to play any games. "You know who. Audra's father."

She blocked out the memory and the pain. That was in her past and she refused to revisit it. The only thing she wanted to do was learn from it. "He didn't hurt me at all. I hurt him."

It was a lie she didn't believe, Will thought, but if it helped her pride to think that he did, there was no harm in it. "I can believe it."

It gave Denise a certain sense of triumph to realize that she could read him like a book. But she didn't care for what she saw on the page. "You're making fun of me."

There was no way to approach this woman without getting her hackles up, Will thought. "Why? Because I said I believed you?"

She hated having her intelligence insulted this way. "Because you don't believe me."

Will looked past his own annoyance. If ever there was a soul in need of comforting, that was hurting, it was hers. He put his arms around her and refused to let her shrug him away, or break out of his hold. He looked down into her face.

"I can understand a man hurting inside when you left him. Hurting so bad that it feels like a knife being stuck into him and twisted slowly. I can understand a man falling so in love with you that he can't think of anything else except wanting you, wanting to make love with you over and over again until nothing else makes sense except having you."

Denise could feel his words, his breath, along her skin. Penetrating her heart. She fought desperately against the feeling. "Stop it."

"Stop what?"

She pressed her lips together, suddenly feeling as if she was going to cry. She did best under adversity, not kindness. Kindness only undermined her and made her melt. "Stop confusing me."

He touched her cheek, cupping it. "How am I confusing you, Denny? Tell me."

One by one, the words seemed to slowly float out of her mouth. "You make me want…"

When she stopped, he coaxed, "What, Denny, what do I make you want?"

It was hard to talk. The words were all sticking to the roof of her mouth. "That's just it, you make me want…and I know I can't…" She looked away. When she looked back at him, her eyes were blazing. "Damn you, Will Cutler, you're messing with my mind."

Will was relieved to hear that. He was beginning to entertain the suspicion that he was dealing with a complete robot.

"And a lovely mind it is, too." He gathered her more closely into his arms until there was very little room between them. "Almost as lovely as your eyes." Lightly he brushed his lips over each lid as they fluttered shut before him. "Almost as lovely as your throat." He pressed a kiss to the slender, long column, noting with pleasure that the pulse there all but danced before him. "But not nearly as lovely as your lips," he whispered just before he kissed her.

Flares. This time, there were definite flares, Denise realized. Flares going off when he kissed her. She was sure of it. Flares that signaled she was in desperate need of help. Help to withstand this onslaught by a man who had no business being in her life. A man who would only complicate things for her.

A man who already *had* complicated things for her.

Unable to help herself, she rose on her toes, her tired body coming alive as she melted against his.

She felt like a nomad in the desert, finally finding the elusive oasis just minutes before she was about to expire.

Denise drank deeply and let it sustain her, all the while knowing that, at best, it was all just a mirage.

7

He drew back and Denise immediately felt as if she was in the middle of parachuting out of a plane when someone had snatched the chute away from her. Suddenly she was plummeting to earth alone and unaided. Unprotected.

Shaken to the bottom of his toes, Will held her face in his hands, gazing at it and desperately trying to get his bearings.

If he wasn't careful…

That was it, he was always careful. Of all the Cutlers, he was the most careful, the most practical. The most clearheaded. And yet, this was *still* happening. He still felt as if he was being turned on his head. Or maybe he was standing upright and the rest of the world had been turned upside down.

Being practical didn't seem to guarantee any sort of immunity against this woman and what she was doing to him. He'd never felt so out of touch with his own sense of control before, as if he had no say in what was happening to him. He'd begun to think that he was never going to have any passionate feelings about a woman, that there would never be one who would leave him wanting.

To discover that he'd been wrong was gratifying. It was also more than a little unsettling to suddenly find himself feeling like an adolescent at the age of thirty-three.

"You are one lethal woman, Denise Cavanaugh. You leave me shaken *and* stirred."

She hadn't seen many movies in her life, but the line was common enough for even her to recognize. It attested to a preference James Bond had. "Like a martini?"

Will smiled, nodding. Wanting to caress her. Wanting to take her right here beneath the stars. Naturally. Like breathing.

But there was nothing natural or soothing about the way he felt. The song about holding onto a tiger by the tail drifted through his mind.

"That would be you," he agreed. "Very heady stuff." He toyed with her hair, slowly sifting a lock of it between his thumb and forefinger. "I'd better take you back before I lose what little sense you've left me."

Inadvertently he'd used almost the exact words that David had once said to her. The sweetness that was reaching out to her was swept away by the bristles of a hard-learned lesson.

Denise stiffened when Will tried to touch her face again.

"And I've got no say in what's happening? You'll just sweep me off my feet and expect me to be blown away by you like some curled up little leaf in the middle of autumn?"

He hadn't a clue where this was coming from, or why. He could only guess that he'd unwittingly triggered a bad memory. He was beginning to hate Audra's father, sight unseen.

"I'm not expecting anything," he retorted, losing his battle with patience before he'd even realized he was engaged in the conflict. "Least of all to have you jump on me when I'm trying to pay you a compliment."

Trying. He was forcing himself to sweet-talk her, Denise realized. Just like David had. And the worst part of it was that it was working. She knew it was because she felt so alone right now, so worried, but that didn't help her block her attraction to Will or stop the feeling from taking possession of her.

"Well, stop trying," she told him coolly. "I'm here for two weeks, that's all. In all likelihood, because you're going to build on the carnival grounds, I probably won't be coming through here next year. And even if I did, by next year you'll probably have a wife or a life, or something to keep you busy and away from me, so why don't you and those lips of yours just back off?"

Angry, she pushed past him and hurried back into the house.

Will stood there, a little stunned, a little dazed. Several half theories notwithstanding, he really wasn't sure just what had happened here. He didn't have a tiger by the tail, it was more like an entire pride of lions.

Emphasis, he thought, on the word pride.

"And that, ladies and gentlemen," he murmured to himself, "is what's called being run over by a freight train."

Because he wasn't entirely sure he could trust himself to be civil to Denise if he ran into her in the house right now, Will waited a few more minutes after he'd reached the house before entering. The only thing he was sure of was that he had never encountered anyone quite like Denise before. Never encountered anyone who made him jump through emotional hoops before.

As of yet, the jury was still out on whether or not that was a good thing.

The grandfather clock in the foyer was just preparing to chime five o'clock the next morning when Denise came down the stairs and into the living room carrying a still partially sleeping Audra in her arms.

She was surprised to find that Will was up ahead of her and appeared ready to go. Recovering quickly, she tried to sound as polite and distant as possible.

Denise shifted Audra up higher in her arms to keep her from slipping. Audra seemed not to notice. "I didn't know whether you were serious about getting an early start."

He unfolded his long legs and rose from the sofa. "I'm usually very serious about the things I say." It was only being around Denise that tended to scramble his composure and thought process.

Usually. Denise latched onto the telltale word. He was probably subtly warning her that when he'd spoken to her last night, he hadn't been serious. In other words, she shouldn't allow herself to feel that there was something evolving between them. Well, at least they agreed. Nothing should be evolving between them. Any sweet talk coming from him was all just part of a game that men played.

But she'd already learned that.

If possible, she stiffened a little more. "I'll keep that in mind."

Will had absolutely no idea what she was trying to communicate with that line. Maybe it was even better that way.

Hearing a noise behind her, Denise turned around. Zoe was smiling at her warmly, gesturing toward the kitchen with a spatula. "Good morning," she called out.

Jake nodded a greeting in Denise's direction as he made his way into the kitchen.

"Don't want it to get cold," he murmured.

"Cold?" Zoe laughed. "It doesn't even have time to hit the plate from the skillet before you eat it. Man thinks it'll hurt my feelings if he chews before swallowing."

Standing like the outsider she was, Denise felt a pang of longing at the love she saw thriving between the older couple. The kind of love that she knew would never be part of her own life. Magical things like all-enduring love just never happened to people like her. She pressed Audra closer to her breast.

"So, what can I get you for breakfast?" Zoe asked, one foot back in the kitchen.

Out of the corner of her eye, Denise saw Jake readily helping himself to a hearty breakfast. He had an appetite like her father used to. When there had been that much on the table to eat.

"Nothing, really," Denise assured the other woman.

A hint of a disapproving frown creased Zoe's lips before she spoke.

"Nonsense, you need to keep your strength up." Sensing further resistance, Zoe leveled a stern look at Denise. "You might as well resign yourself to the fact that you are not leaving here until I see you eat something."

Will was beside Denise. "Better listen to her."

There was affection in his voice as he glanced at his mother. "She might look like a pushover, but she ruled us with an iron hand. Still does." Looking down into Denise's eyes, he winked at her.

A wave of queasiness came on response. Her empty stomach had nothing to do with it. "All right," she surrendered. "Toast."

"On the side." Zoe counternegotiated with a decisive nod of her head. "Come on, child, let's get you off to a proper start."

For an inkling of a moment, as Zoe led her off, Denise felt as if she was twelve again. She had to admit, at least to herself, that it wasn't an entirely unpleasant sensation.

Denise looked at Will as he turned off the engine after pulling into a parking space in the visitors section of the hospital parking lot. "What are you doing?"

Unbuckling his seat belt, he pocketed the car key. "Parking the car."

She didn't want him to think he had to accompany her into the building, or wait until she got inside. "You don't have to. Audra and I can walk from here by ourselves."

Will got out, then rounded the hood in time to open the rear passenger door for Audra. The little girl fairly bounced out of the car.

"I have no concern about you walking, Denise,"

he said matter-of-factly, taking Audra's hand in his. "I figure you've been doing it long enough to get it right. I'm coming with you."

She didn't like the way Audra gravitated toward him instead of her. She didn't want to have to wean her daughter's affection away from Will. Or deal with the pieces once they were on the road again.

Puzzled by his motives, Denise studied his face. "Why?"

He was already walking toward the hospital. Denise had no choice but to keep up. "To see how your father's doing."

The man's legs were much too long, Denise thought. She found she had to hurry in order just to keep pace. "I repeat, why?"

Will waited for Denise to catch up at the curb, then walked through the electronic doors with Audra. "Why are you so suspicious?"

He wasn't supposed to be the one asking questions, she was. "I find it easier that way. No surprises."

The lobby of the hospital was warm and inviting just the way he'd meant it to be, Will noted with a small sense of pride. There was nothing threatening or forbidding about it as hospitals had once been.

"Surprises are part of the nicer things in life," he told Denise.

Surprises usually meant something had gone

wrong, or something bad was about to happen. "Not as far as I'm concerned."

Audra tugged on his arm. "I like surprises," she told him when he looked down at her.

He'd take support any way he could find it. Will scooped her up in his arms as if she weighed next to nothing. She almost did.

"Girl after my own heart," he teased affection ately. And, if he were being honest, she'd already won it. It had to be a family trait, he decided.

Audra's mouth formed an almost perfect O as she looked at him in confused surprise. "I'm not after your heart, Will."

"Well, too bad, you've got it anyway." Giving her a huge bear hug, he set her down on the floor again. "All right, ladies, let's get the show on the road." He saw the puzzled frown on Audra's face. "Figure of speech, honey."

Audra's eyes danced with laughter she hadn't let loose yet. "You talk funny."

"Sometimes," he agreed. And then he looked over Audra's head at Denise. "And as to why, I thought maybe your father could do with a little en couragement since you seem bent on seeing only the dark side."

Denise was about to snap that he could leave her father to her, but bit back the retort. He was trying to do a good deed, even though she had no idea why. There wasn't anything in it for him.

"That's very nice of you," she finally guardedly allowed.

He began to lead them to the elevators on the side. "Haven't you noticed? I'm a nice guy."

"Yes," Denise muttered under her breath, "I've noticed."

The grin on Will's face as they entered the elevator told her that he'd heard her.

It was a spacious, bright-looking waiting area, designed to help soothe the frayed nerves of those who occupied it. Denise felt agitated the moment she entered it. Having Will sitting beside her didn't help her state of mind.

Rising, she went to stand by the window. It looked out on the open field behind the hospital. She stared at it without seeing. Her mind was on what was happening within the operating room not thirty feet away. Glancing up, she saw Will's reflection in the glass. He was reading to Audra. She struggled against slipping into the warm, comfortable place that yawned before her. It was only an illusion. She knew that.

"You don't have to stay here, you know."

Marking his place, Will looked up. Her back was tense, he thought. It bothered him that there was nothing he could do to help her. "I know."

She swung around, spoiling for a fight. Wanting to tear into something. Anything to take her mind off the operation. Off the fears dancing around her like a bedeviled witch doctor in an old Saturday morning cliffhanger.

"Then why are you?"

He placed the book on Audra's lap and rose. Crossing to Denise, he placed a hand on her shoulder. She wasn't tense, she was rigid. "Because I think you could use a hand to hold."

"Mama can hold my hand," Audra volunteered.

Turning, Will smiled at the little girl. "Of course she can." He looked at Denise. "I meant a large hand." He closed his hand over hers.

Against her better instincts, Denise left her hand where it was, at least for a moment. She couldn't have said why it felt comforting to have this man holding her hand, but it did.

But because it did, she forced herself to pull her hand away. She looked at the time. Ten minutes since the last time she'd stared at the clock. "I thought you said you had to go to work."

Will shook his head. "No, you said that. I decided to call in and take a few days off." He smiled into her eyes. There was vulnerability there. He wondered what she would say if she knew he'd seen through her facade. "I've got a lot of vacation time stored up, but until today, I really haven't seen the need to take any."

"Need?" She pounced on the word as if it had reared its head and bitten her.

"Wrong word." He realized his error. She probably thought that he meant he needed to comfort her. Denise obviously thought that being occasionally needy meant being weak. "Desire," Will amended.

Desire.

The word rippled along her skin as if it were a seductive whisper.

Here she was, in a hospital waiting area, anticipating the outcome of her father's surgery, her daughter sitting not five fidgety feet away from her and she was actually allowing herself to be affected by a man who had been a total stranger less than forty-eight hours ago.

Damn, but she should have her head examined. And her heart permanently excised.

"As long as you want to hang around…"

"Yes?" he coaxed when she let her voice trail off.

She nodded toward Audra. "You might as well finish reading that story to Audra."

Will grinned as he turned to look at Audra. "I never could resist a captivating smile." Crossing back to the sofa, he picked up the book and resumed reading.

Denise turned away and went back to looking out the window. The sound of his voice was a soothing cushion for her agitated thoughts.

"You're humming." Will couldn't help the amazement in his voice.

"Yes, I'm humming." She would have been singing if she could carry a tune. The surgery had gone well and everything looked upbeat for a change.

"Are you happy, Mama?" Audra struggled against the seat belt that was buckled around her lap, trying to lean forward.

Denise half turned in her seat. "Yes, I'm happy, baby. Grampa's going to be just fine."

"Just like Will promised," Audra reminded her loyally.

For once, she didn't feel like arguing. "Yes, just like Will promised." Her eyes shifted toward him. "Got any more promises you want to keep?"

"A few," he said significantly.

"I wish..."

"What do you wish?" he coaxed when Denise didn't finish.

But her courage was gone and with it, the moment. "I wish I didn't have to work today."

He had a strong feeling that wasn't what she'd wanted to say, but he let it pass.

"I'll help you, Mama."

"Like you always do, baby, like you always do," she murmured with affection.

"Looks like you have a welcoming committee," he commented. Several of the crew members were gathered at the entrance to the grounds.

"Uh-oh," she murmured. The euphoria, she

thought with a pang, had been short-lived. Time to return to the real world.

"Hey, Denise, where've you been?" the tallest of the men demanded, striding toward the car as soon as Will parked it. Thin and wiry, Skip looked to be solid muscle despite his frame. Both eyebrows knit together to form a single dark, angry line. He looked into the interior of the car. "And where's Tate?"

She wasn't accustomed to having to account for herself, especially to someone who worked for her. "He's in the hospital. It's a long story," she said quickly to forestall any questions. She had one of her own. "What's the matter?" Skip wouldn't have been standing around, waiting for her if everything was going well.

He didn't bother with a preamble. "Todd and Angel quit this morning."

The words felt like two sharp knives slashing away at her strength. "Why?" She looked from one man to another, looking for an answer.

Skip said nothing, but the man next to him, Roy, told her. "They said it was a long time in coming. When Jules left," he mentioned the last man to quit just before they came to Serendipity, "that started them thinking that maybe they should find something else to do, too. And then Harry left yesterday. Todd and Angel said there was no future in staying here."

Momentarily stymied, she blew out a breath.

What next? "Great, four people in one month." She thought of her father. He hadn't been able to help putting the structures up, but he still ran the carousel, at least in theory. For the sake of his pride, even though he was absent, she amended the count. "Five."

Roy looked at her, concern in his dark brown eyes. "What are we going to do, Denise? We can't be everywhere at once. And how are we going to finish putting up the rides and testing them? Cecil and me—" he nodded at the man behind him "—have been working since sunup, but—"

"I know you have." She bit her lip, thinking. There was no way she could afford to lose this job and she knew that postponing it was out of the question. The carnival was slated to open tomorrow. More than three-quarters of the trade booths were already up. She turned toward Will. "Is there anywhere I can go to get some manpower in a hurry?"

Will nodded. Finally she was asking him for help—at least in a roundabout way. "Yeah, there's somewhere you can go."

"Where?"

He reached into the Jeep and took his cell phone out of the glove compartment. "Let me make a few calls."

"I'd appreciate it. Oh, and one more thing—find people who'll work cheap. I'll be over by the Ferris wheel." She looked and saw that the ride was yet to be completely assembled. Denise sighed, walking off.

He nodded, waiting for the person on the other end to pick up.

Finishing his last call, Will flipped the cover on his cell phone, closing it. He looked over toward the Ferris wheel. Most of the seats had been attached, but what caught his attention was Denise. She was about ten feet off the ground, climbing up through the network of newly erected steel.

He stood back for a moment, watching her work. How could anyone who moved as agilely as a spider monkey look so damn sexy while she was doing it?

Afraid of distracting Denise, he approached the Ferris wheel without calling to her. She saw him just as he reached the foot of the structure.

Denise tightened her hold on a beam. "Any luck?" she called down to him.

"Plenty." Cupping his mouth, he raised his voice to be heard above the noise. "All good. Help is on its way."

It sounded like a rallying cry, Denise thought. For the second time that day, she breathed a sigh of relief.

With sure movements, she made her way back down to the ground.

"It's fine." She directed her approval to the man setting up the ticket booth beside the ride. Brushing off her hands, she looked at Will. "Who did you get, or shouldn't I ask?"

Instead of answering her, Will placed his hand on her shoulder and turned her toward the official police vehicle that was pulling into the lot. "Here's the first of them, now."

She didn't understand. "You called the sheriff?"

"No," Will explained mildly, "I called my brother Quint."

Her eyes widened at the information. "The sheriff's your brother?"

Had she waited a minute longer, Denise realized she wouldn't have had to ask that question. The resemblance between the two men as the sheriff approached was unmistakable. Even more evident than the resemblance between Will and Kent. All three brothers were blond, tall and well muscled, with skin bronzed from years of working outdoors and eyes the color of the sky that looked down at them.

Her mouth curved as she turned to look at Will. "Did your mother have access to a photocopier when she first married your father?"

Will laughed. "We don't look *that* much alike."

If he believed that, he was blind. "Yeah, you do," she insisted.

Audra, who had been hanging around him all this time, waiting for Will to finish his calls and pay attention to her now smiled at him loyally. "I think you're the best-looking one."

Unable to resist, he scooped Audra up into his arms. It amazed him that he could lose his heart to someone so little so quickly.

"Thank you. And I think you're the best-looking one here." He kissed her cheek, then looked at Denise. "You have the makings of a first-class flirt on your hands."

Denise laughed, the worried expression on her face softening slightly. For now, help was at hand. She'd deal with the rest of it later.

"You know, Cutler, I think you might finally be right about something."

He had a feeling that he was right about more than just one thing, Will thought, looking at Denise, but he kept that to himself.

At least for the time being.

8

→ —— ←

Denise felt her heart slipping away from her.

It would have been something to enjoy, to treasure, if reality hadn't been standing beside her, ready to poke sharp, bony fingers into every dream, every feeling that rose like a sparkling soap bubble in the air, rainbows dancing along its fragile surface. Reality that was quick to cruelly remind her what had happened the last time she'd lost the reins holding her heart in check.

And the way it had felt after. After the lights of the party had gone out.

After the lights in David's eyes had gone out. And she was left to grope around in the dark and cope with the results of being head-over-heels in love. To cope with being pregnant and emotionally abandoned.

She tried to remember all that. But it didn't help much.

She watched Will work beneath the hot sun, sweat

gleaming along his tanned skin, a slick badge attesting to his efforts. To his work.

There was a difference, she thought, trying to hold onto the ember of warmth glowing within her breast. A difference between the two men. David had dazzled her with his world; Will had quietly brought his world into hers.

Well, maybe not so quietly, she amended as the noise around her seemed to swell and grow as she crossed over to Will. She heard him begin to swear roundly when Quint bumped into him, nearly throwing him off-kilter, then swallow the words as he looked to see if Audra was around.

Her heart slipped away a little further.

"You're making me feel guilty."

The slight breeze shifted a second before she approached. Will caught the light, tantalizing scent and knew she was behind him before Denise had said a word. "About?"

He and his brothers and father had been at it for the last four hours. "You're all working so hard and I can't pay any of you." She'd never liked that, owing someone. Even if it made the difference between getting along or not, she always wanted to have her tab paid. How was she ever going to repay this family for their help and their kindness? It didn't seem possible.

"No need to pay us, darlin'," Quint interjected.

Coming up on her other side, Quint gently nudged

Denise out of the way and plunged his hand into the ice chest. He groped around the melting shavings, searching for a can of cola.

"We're doing it as a favor to Will." Quint grinned at his brother before continuing. "We like having him owe us. Nice to be on the other side of the fence for a change." He winked at Denise, popping the top off the prize he snared. Quint drank deeply, finishing the can in four long pulls.

"Don't pay attention to him," Will told her. He wiped his damp forehead with the back of his hand. "If the pack of them did favors for me from now until the turn of the century, they wouldn't even scratch the surface of what they owe me."

Quint sighed, throwing the empty can into the large barrel that one of the carnival committee members had set up for recyclables. It pinged as it came to rest on top of the other cans.

"The sad part of that is, it's true." Quint glanced at his watch, gauging his schedule. "I've only got ninety minutes left," he told Denise, beginning to head back to the ride he was putting up with Kent and two of Denise's people. "If I stay away any longer than that, Carly's liable to lock himself up in the jail by accident." He laughed, thinking of his cousin, who was also his deputy. The man was very willing, but not too able.

Will turned to look at Denise. The furrow between her brows was beginning to fade, he noted, pleased. "Where do you want me?"

Denise blinked, the question taking her completely by surprise. And creating some rather unsubtle responses that she kept to herself. "Excuse me?"

Amusement curved his mouth and she had a feeling he knew the exact wording of every response that had occurred to her. The flush on her cheeks was half embarrassment, half face-saving anger.

"Well, I'm finished with the miniature train ride." He nodded toward the circle of open red railway cars. "Where do you want me to go next?"

Denise decided it was best to simply ignore his grin, its source and its engaging effect. She looked around the grounds. "The carousel still needs work." She pointed toward it.

"The carousel it is." He began to walk off, then stopped, a thought occurring to him. "How long have you been working carnivals, Denny?"

It wasn't so much a matter of working them as living them. "I was born in the Fortune Teller's tent." Denise saw the skepticism in his eyes. He probably thought she was exaggerating. "My mother didn't realize she was in labor until it was too late." Her hands went automatically to her hips. "Why?"

Was it his imagination, or did she always look as if she was ready to forge into battle at the slightest provocation? "When was the last time you enjoyed the carnival?"

He'd answered her question with a question, Denise realized. Typical. "I don't follow you."

Will spelled it out for her, his curiosity urging him on. "When was the last time you went on any of the rides, had cotton candy? Like a 'townie'?"

He enunciated the word as if it described an undesirable, Denise thought, flushing. He must have overheard her. "I don't know. A year or two..." It annoyed her that his scrutinizing gaze had her shifting self-consciously. "About five," she amended grudgingly.

Will had his doubts about that. He raised one eyebrow dubiously. "Maybe longer?" he suggested.

"Maybe." She didn't have time to stand around and argue over something that was none of his business. "What's your point?"

He grinned, pleased with his inspirational idea. "My point is, I know how you can repay me."

"How? Extra tickets? Because if it's extra tickets, I've already seen to it that your family—"

But he shook his head, taking away some of her thunder. He held up one finger. "Just one extra one—for you if you need it."

Something shaky began to form within her, crawling out from between the chinks that existed in the stone wall that had been around her now errant heart. She licked her lower lip. "I don't understand…"

Yes, she did. Will could see it in her eyes. But he told her anyway so that there were no excuses, no feigned misunderstandings as to his intent.

"I want to take you to the carnival, Denny, as soon as you can spare the time." He caught her hand in his, surprised at his own enthusiasm. And pleased by it. "I want you to see the magic again, not just the grease and wrenches."

Don't do this to me, heart. Don't let me start believing him.

She drew her hand away, pocketing it. "Don't you have anyone else you want to bring?"

Will didn't move an inch. Holding his ground, holding her attention, he looked into her eyes.

"No," he said with a note of finality that rippled along her skin. "I don't."

Run, damn it. Run for your life.

Denise's own urgings fell on ears that couldn't hear. She looked away, lifting her shoulder in a half shrug. "All right, when I can spare the time. If I'm not too exhausted."

He gave her a knowing look, then laughed. "Oh, you won't be too exhausted, Denny. That would mean you're human, and I don't think you're quite ready to admit to something like that."

He knew her better than she wanted him to. There was no way she could honestly argue with his assessment. So, in retaliation, she grabbed a handful of ice from the chest and tossed it at him. Surprised, Will yelped as the cold chips hit him on the chest and slid down.

"Of course you know this means war—and I'm a veteran of a lot more ferocious attacks than that." His eyes dancing, he took a large handful of ice, throwing it at her.

Using both hands, she scooped up a huge mound and flung it at him, aiming for his face.

Will had had years of practice, thanks to his brothers and sister. Ducking his head, he hooked his arm around her waist, pulling her to him. Will dipped into the quickly depleting supply of ice with the other and brought up a huge handful.

Her eyes trained on the cold mound, she squirmed against him. "Oh, you wouldn't." Laughter robbed her voice of its proper conviction.

"Wouldn't I?"

His eyes were unreadable. The next minute, a tiny glob of ice was sliding down her back. She shrieked, laughter rocking her, vibrating her body against his.

"Stop it," she begged, trying to wiggle away.

He surprised Denise by turning her around to face him, his arm still tightly wrapped around her waist. "Ask me nicely."

What breath the laughter hadn't robbed her of evaporated now. There was barely enough left to sustain her.

"Please?" She squeezed out the request.

His arm slipped away, releasing her. He didn't have to physically restrain her. His smile held her in place far more firmly than his arm could. "Never could resist a lady with manners."

Kiss me, Will. Kiss me before I have sense enough to break away.

"Mama, are you all right?"

Rescued, by a pint-size intruder, Denise thought. Just in time. She looked toward Audra, a sad smile playing along her lips. "I'm fine, honey."

Audra looked from her mother to Will and back again. He could see by her expression that her loyalties were clearly torn. "But what was he doing to you?"

"Here, I'll show you," Will told her. The very next minute, he took just the tiniest sliver of ice and slid it down the back of the little girl's T-shirt.

Squealing with delight, Audra giggled and squirmed. What was left of the ice chip shimmied from underneath her T-shirt and plodded like a large teardrop to the ground beside her feet. She was instantly enamored with the new game.

"This is fun!"

Will looked at Denise over Audra's head. "Yes," he agreed softly, his eyes on Denise's. "It is."

Denise fervently wished that her heart wasn't hammering as if she'd just run half a mile to get in out of the rain.

* * *

Her feet aching, Denise dropped to one of the benches the carnival committee had supplied. She sighed, wishing she could toe off her boots.

She'd put him off for almost a full week, using one excuse after another. But finally she was out of excuses and out of defenses. She allowed him to take her to the carnival. Like a townie.

Will slid into the seat beside her. He resisted the temptation to slip his arm around her. Progress was made in small steps, not huge leaps. The latter he left for his heart.

"Is that a tired sigh or a contented sigh?" he asked her.

She took a deep breath and let it out again before answering. No sense in letting him know just how happy she felt right now—although she had the uneasy suspicion that he already knew. Looking straight ahead of her, Denise said, "Both. I've been so busy trying to make ends meet, worrying about maintaining the crew and the equipment that I overlooked the real reason the carnival exists in the first place."

Will leaned forward to see her face. They'd taken in every ride twice and he'd plied her with pink cotton candy and hot dogs. "So you're having fun."

Denise could feel her mouth curving. She just couldn't help herself.

"Yes, I'm having fun." Her hair rained over her

face as she leaned forward, tilting her head. She looked at him. "Isn't it obvious?"

He laughed softly. All around them, twilight was tiptoeing in like a reluctant adolescent, wanting to eke out just a few more minutes before curfew. Will gave in to temptation and slipped his arm around her shoulders.

"Nothing about you is obvious, Denny. That's why I ask questions."

For just a moment, Denise allowed herself to enjoy the contact and laid her head against his shoulder. She glanced up toward the sky. Was it her imagination, or were the stars coming out already? "It was nice of your mother to look after Audra tonight and your father to run one of the booths."

"I come from nice people." His breath feathered along her hair.

If only there was a way to bottle moments and capture them forever. This was the one she'd pick. The one she'd keep and take out to look at on those occasional evenings when she was feeling lost and alone.

"They really are," she agreed. "Your whole family's nice."

He laughed and she raised her head to look at him. "You haven't met Hank and Morgan."

"No, I haven't."

And it bothered her that she probably wouldn't.

It bothered her even more that when she moved on, she was going to remember this man.

And miss him.

That wasn't good. Not in the long run. But maybe caring a little about one man would prevent her from ever fatally falling for another.

A smile teased the corners of her mouth as she thought about it. It was like getting a tiny bit of the flu to act as a vaccine against coming down with the disease in earnest.

Will felt her smile more than saw it. Sliding his knuckles against her cheek, he turned her face toward his. "What are you thinking about?"

"Flu vaccines. And you." The latter admission slipped out.

He shook his head. "I won't ask the connection. Something tells me I'd rather not know." In the distance, he heard one of the bands starting a set. He rose, coaxing her to her feet. "So, what's next?"

"Next?" We've been going on rides for the last three hours."

The music was growing louder. He could feel it in his body, making his toe tap. "We've hardly scratched the surface. The shows are going to start now."

Denise had seen the flyer. There were at least fifteen different programs, from the 4-H Club to a senior citizens' quartet singing songs from the Big Band era, slated for the evenings.

"Ah, yes, the local talent."

He raised a bemused brow. "Do I detect a note of snobbery?" he teased.

She'd had to endure some pretty dreadful performances in her time. Even if she wasn't watching, she could still hear. "Well..."

Will began drawing her toward the nearest stage. "Hey, all talent has to be local to somewhere. Tell you what, if the show's bad, we can leave and find another one to listen to."

"And if I said no?" she challenged, not because she wanted to be stubborn, but just because she wanted to hear what he'd say.

"I'm bigger than you are," he deadpanned. "The sheriff's my brother. You won't say no."

She was being charmed again and she knew it. But knowing still didn't help her resist. She shrugged goodnaturedly. "Then I won't."

He kissed her cheek quickly. "Love a cooperative woman," he said before drawing her to the first stage.

She could feel the outline of his lips far longer than she knew was safe.

The first show he lured her to was a ventriloquist act. She found herself laughing and willing to suspend disbelief long enough to enjoy the wise cracks of the wooden partner on the performer's knee.

There was a singing group on the second makeshift stage and a band playing bluegrass music on the third. She was more than willing to listen to it, but when Will began to lead her to where other couples were dancing, she dug in her heels and hung back.

Will looked at her quizzically. "What's the matter?"

"They're dancing," she stated needlessly.

"Yes, they are." He waited for her to say something further. "So?" he asked when she didn't. And then suddenly he knew. "You don't dance, do you?"

If he laughed, she was going to hit him. "Never exactly had time to learn."

"You've got the time now."

She stiffened, ready to turn on her heel and walk away at the slightest hint of the wrong answer. "You're not going to—"

"Yes, I am." Refusing to take no for an answer, Will held her hand firmly and drew her toward the other dancing couples.

The evening had gone too nicely to cause a scene now, but she didn't want to dance. "No, really, I've got two left feet."

He spared her a glance. The appraisal in his eyes sent a silent shiver through her.

"The last time I looked, everything you had was in exactly the right place, in exactly the right proportions." He saw the resistance in her countenance.

He bent his head. "Remember," he whispered against her ear, "you owe me—"

Denise tried not to react to his breath on her skin. "So do your brothers."

He laughed, not about to be talked or coerced out of it. "They can't dance worth a lick."

Her chin shot up. "Neither can I."

"Maybe," he allowed amiably, "but you're a lot softer to hold than Quint is."

His arms were already around her. Denise found herself trapped within a well-muscled prison with no hope for escape. The only course left open to her was to seek parole for good behavior. That meant allowing herself to be humiliated.

Will could read her mind. It amazed him how in-tune he was to her and how quickly that had all happened.

"Look around you," he prompted. When she did, he said, "Nobody's watching you, they're having too good a time themselves. The only one who's going to be looking at you is me, and I'm already doing that."

He was wearing her down, Denise thought. Not that she had all that much choice in the matter. "You're going to be sorry."

"Let me worry about that."

The band struck up a new song, something lively and vibrant. Denise gave up protesting. If he wanted to have his feet mashed, that was his choice. "You asked for this."

"Yes, I guess I did." But he wasn't sorry.

Not even after she'd stomped on his foot a third time. Embarrassed, Denise flushed, trying to pull away. "I think we should quit while you can still walk."

Will had no intention of quitting. The only thing he was intent on was enjoying Denise. He tightened his arms around her.

"If I fall, you'll hold me up."

The look in her eyes mocked him. "You have a lot of faith in me."

"No, actually I have a lot of faith in me—and my ability to judge people."

"There's no arguing with you, is there?"

If ever there was a case of the pot calling the kettle black, this had to be it, he thought. "No, but I've got a feeling that you're surely going to try anyway, aren't you?"

"What do you think?"

Instead of answering, Will laughed and spun her around again. He knew exactly what to think. And right now, the prospect of arguing with her until doomsday didn't bother him a bit.

9

Even the air smelled sweeter tonight. Denise took a deep breath, trying to sustain the evening, sorry that it was over. Will had made her forget for a little while. Forget everything but him.

She turned toward him now in front of her trailer. Will's mother was inside, and she knew the woman had to be anxious to get home. No one stayed in a place like this if they had somewhere better to go. Like a house that sat in the midst of acres of land like a delicate bloom on top of a hearty cactus.

Funny how that seemed appealing to her now.

"I've forgotten how much fun going to the carnival can be. Thank you."

Will decided that he loved her smile—not just liked, but loved. It lit up her entire face, erasing all the signs of tension. He wished there was some way to prolong the evening. And make it the beginning of many evenings to come.

"I think you've forgotten how to have fun, period."

"Maybe." Denise tried not to think about how close he was standing to her, or how much closer she would have liked him to be. She knew where that led. And where that ended. "There's not much fun to be had these days, not with the business shrinking the way it is." Saying that almost made her feel guilty for having this evening when everything was so bleak for her and the others. "Every time I turn around, something else needs to be fixed, or replaced or Audra's outgrown her clothes again."

"Or your father's getting sick," Will interjected softly. He slipped his arm around her and noticed that this time, she didn't stiffen. "How long has he been this way?"

"Sickly?" She shut her eyes, suddenly weary. "Longer than I care to admit." Denise rallied, opening her eyes again. She wasn't going to let herself grow melancholy in front of him. That was no way to pay him back for tonight. "I couldn't seem to bully him into going to see a doctor."

He laughed softly. "Well, if you couldn't do it, then it couldn't be done. Don't beat yourself up over it."

She wasn't accustomed to being comforted. She was accustomed to being the one doing the comforting. "I don't know whether to thank you for trying to ease my conscience, or to hit you for making a crack."

He had no doubt that she wasn't kidding. "Do I get to vote?"

A feeling of magnanimity governed her tonight. Maybe it was the cotton candy. Unused to indulging, she was probably on the verge of overdosing on sugar. "Sure, why not?"

Maneuvering her against the back of the trailer, Will framed her body with his arms. "Then I'm going to write in my own candidate."

Denise liked the way he talked. Every time she thought he was strictly down to earth, he turned flowery on her. "Which is?"

When he held her this way, her body fit neatly against his. Even more closely than it had when they were dancing. It was the way he liked it. "If you can't guess by now, lady, then you're not nearly as sharp as I think you are."

Longing rippled through her, deep and insistent. She almost gave in. As it was, she allowed herself to linger a second longer on its brink than she knew was safe.

"Oh, but I am. Sharper. So sharp that I know that it's for the best that I don't let this go any further than it's gone already."

Cocking his head, he studied her face. "Doesn't sound very sharp to me."

Denise pushed away from him. She needed space between them if she was going to say this. She didn't know why she wanted to, but she did.

"The summer I turned nineteen, we passed through a town that was just north of Monterey, California. Silverton."

She said the name as if there was a world full of memories attached to it, Will thought. He experienced the very first prick of jealousy he'd ever felt. It took effort not to say anything and to refrain from taking her back into his arms. But he knew she couldn't be crowded. What he took to be comfort, she understood as being possessed and controlled. Putting his own feelings aside, he gave Denise her space.

"They were putting on a charity benefit, a real big deal and they wanted rides, lots of rides." She pressed her lips together, determined not to allow the memory to burrow its way through. "I lost my heart on one of those rides." Her mouth curved in a self-deprecating smile. "Lost a lot more than that, although not directly on the ride." Though she was trying not to let it, a tiny patch of the past was calling to her, coaxing her back. Trying to stir up her feelings.

Denise struggled to keep her voice matter-of-fact, but it wasn't easy. "His name was David Donnelly, and he looked as if he'd stepped out of a dream. He was tall, dark and had the nicest smile. He charmed me right out of my boots." She laughed shortly, looking away. "Out of a few other things, too. It was a beautiful summer romance."

She glanced at the side of the trailer, where their logo was written in huge, fading script letters, as if seeing it somehow grounded her.

"We were on our way to Galveston when I realized that there was one more of us than had originally signed on." Now there was no stopping them. The feelings she'd experienced then were all coming back to her. Not the love, but the aftermath. The emptiness and pain. She blew out a breath. "I was scared and excited at the same time. I was naive enough to think that the baby I was carrying was the physical embodiment of the love I actually thought existed between David and me. I was set straight quickly enough. The letter I wrote him eventually found its way back to me, marked 'Return To Sender, Address Unknown.'

"Address Unknown," she repeated with a shake of her head. There was no humor in it, but the joke, cruel and painful, had been on her. "His family had the biggest house in the valley. I really don't think the mail carrier had trouble finding it." She shoved fisted hands into her jeans. "So I got my courage up and called from the first town we hit. The maid told me he wasn't taking calls from strangers." Tears were shimmering in her eyes when she looked at Will. She felt them and damned herself for them. Only small children and fools cried, and she wasn't a small child anymore. "I told her to tell him that he was going to be a father. I never heard from him." She pressed her lips together. "So, you see why I don't want this going anywhere."

Unable to hold back any longer, Will cupped her cheek. It was damp. Sympathy and anger rose up, twins born of the same moment.

"No, I don't see," he said softly, wiping away the tear that trickled down with his thumb. "What I see is a woman who's bitten into one rotten apple and condemned the whole orchard."

The comparison made Denise laugh. And gave her the opportunity to get a grip on herself. For a moment, she allowed herself to absorb the comfort he'd silently offered, then slowly moved her head away. "So now you're an apple?"

"I'll be anything you want, as long as it makes that look in your eyes go away."

Painfully aware of what he saw, she still managed to lift her chin defiantly. "What look?"

"The sad one."

Denise opened her mouth to retort that he was imagining things, then stopped. He'd shown her a nice time tonight. He didn't deserve to be repaid with a lie. Wasn't that why she'd told him about David in the first place? So he could understand?

A smile flirted with her lips. "You do drive a hard bargain, Will Cutler."

Will took her face between his hands and kissed her so softly, she felt her soul aching. And melting away from her as quickly as a block of ice left un-attended in the July sun.

She sighed against his lips. "A damn hard bargain."

"I always was the smart one in my family," he murmured before his lips took hers again, this time with far more feeling, far more enthusiasm.

She clung to the kiss, to promises she knew couldn't be fulfilled. Clung to him because, just for a moment, she pretended that he was the fantasy prince she'd once believed David to be.

But fantasy princes were all just that—fantasy. And she had a six-year-old daughter, an ailing father and a failing business to see to. Reality allowed fantasy a very short shelf life.

"I'd better go and relieve your mother."

He closed his hand over hers, holding her in place a second longer. "I don't think she'll be all that relieved. My mother dotes on anyone under four feet. I know she loves looking after Audra."

Denise stood up on her toes, her mouth tantalizingly close to his. "If you're trying to talk me into leaving Audra with your mother a while longer and going off with you..."

"Yes?" he asked encouragingly.

She drew her hand away and patted his chest. "You should save that sweet talk and use it on someone who counts."

"I am," he said as she turned to walk inside. "And you do."

She didn't turn around. "Don't say that," she ordered, disappearing inside.

"Even if I didn't," Will said to the emptiness that took her place, "it wouldn't make it any less true."

He sighed and shoved his hands into his pockets, turning away.

"Why, Will, did you wait out here to walk me to your father's booth?"

Will smiled, offering his mother his arm as she stepped out of the trailer. "Can't have my best girl walking around in the dark by herself."

Zoe touched his cheek. Will was the one who had never given her a moment's concern, who had always been there, ready and willing to help without a complaint on his lips. She'd known almost from the moment he was born that he had a heart of gold.

She wished she could protect it now, but he was a grown man and there wasn't anything she could do. Except love him.

"Your best girl sees right through you, Will Alan Cutler," she told him as they walked through the grounds. "She'll come around."

"Don't know what you're talking about, Mom."

"Uh-huh." Zoe waited a beat before saying, "Audra's crazy about you. That's half the battle."

"Not for a woman who thrives on war," he replied, more to himself than to her.

* * *

"I don't need you tagging along all the time. Don't you have a boss somewhere, getting mad because you're never there?"

Denise glared at Will who had insisted on accompanying her to the hospital. After the other night, he'd shown up on the grounds the next day, acting as if nothing out of the ordinary had happened between them. And continued to act that way. Which was just the way she'd wanted it.

Or thought she did until it actually went that way. Then it bothered her that he hadn't thought their night at the carnival was anything more than just a few pleasant hours. She'd bared some of her soul to him, for crying out loud. Didn't that mean anything to him?

But just as she'd shored up her beaches again, he'd appeared before her trailer door this morning, announcing that he was going to take her to the hospital to pick up her father who was finally being released today.

She hadn't said a word to him about that. How did he even know her father was supposed to come home?

Grudgingly, because part of her did welcome his company and his moral support, she finally got into Will's car and allowed him to drive her to the hospital.

In an odd sort of way, Will was getting used to

her suspicions and having her question his every move. Funny how quickly that had fallen into place.

Just as quickly as his feelings for her had.

"You'd make a wonderful truant officer, Denise." He drove past one of Serendipity's three elementary schools. The newest one that he had helped design. It started him thinking. "Speaking of truant, what do you do about Audra's schooling during the year?"

What gave him the right to think he could just pry into her affairs as if she'd invited him to do so?

"I take care of it." The dubious look he gave her galvanized her defenses into place. "If it's any business of yours, I took all the tests and got the necessary papers to allow me to conduct her classes at home. Audra already knows more about geography than the average adult," she told him proudly. "And she learned how to read when she was four. Dad's in charge of teaching her the finer points of math and she knows all the parts required to put together a first-class Ferris wheel. I'd say she was getting a damn fine education, thank you for asking."

Will laughed, slowly easing the car around the next corner. "I don't think I've ever been thanked with quite that much venom before." He spared her a glance. "Don't know why I keep coming back for more." Yeah, he did, he thought. Knew damn well why.

She took offense at the teasing remark because it

was easier to deal with it that way than to let it hurt. "That makes two of us. I can't seem to get rid of you."

He stopped at one of the few lights. "Do you really want to?"

No, she didn't and that was what was wrong. "I already told you, this isn't going to go anywhere."

"You didn't answer my question. Do you really want me to go?"

If he wanted to hear her say that she wanted him to stay, he had a long wait ahead of him. But she wasn't going to lie outright, either. "No, not yet I suppose. Your family's coming in very handy."

The light turned green, and he took his foot off the brake. "So, you want me for my family. The least you could say was that you wanted me for my body."

She was trying very hard *not* to want him for his body—among other things—and not succeeding very well at it. "Why, is that what they usually say?"

"*They?*"

The quick shrug was meant to reek of indifference. "The other women you've been with."

Will saw no reason for games. "As all my brothers will gladly tell you at the least possible provocation, the last female's company I enjoyed was the family dog, Queenie. I was always too busy to think about relationships and socializing.'' Taking another turn, he drove onto the hospital lot.

Denise couldn't see how that was possible. Not with his looks and certainly not with his manner. To put icing on the cake, the man was a professional. He had everything going for him. How could there not be women in his life? There had been in David's. Even while she was offering him her soul, there'd been someone else in the wings. That's just the way men were.

She got out of the car before he could open the door for her. ''And you're suddenly not too busy?''

What did it take to convince this woman that he wasn't like the last man in her life? Will thought. ''Hell, yes. But that doesn't seem to make a difference when it comes to you.'' The electronic doors of the pristine blue-and-white building opened to admit them. ''The day I was making the presentation—the day you ran me off the road—all I could think about was you.''

''I did *not* run you off the road,'' she insisted heatedly. But a touch of vanity goaded her into asking, ''Why?'' as they walked into the elevator.

He knew what she was asking. Will pressed for the second floor. ''Damned if I know. But I haven't been able to get you out of my mind since.''

She didn't know what to say to that. Didn't know how to feel about that. Other than afraid.

The doors opened again and Will ushered her toward the nurses' station, a tiny desk that was littered with patients' charts and an army of inexpensive black pens, all without their caps on.

The nurse at the desk looked up as they approached. Will didn't recognize her. "We're here to take Mr. Cavanaugh home."

Denise was about to inform him that she was perfectly able to sign her father out herself, but what the nurse said in response stopped her.

"Certainly." She plucked Tate's chart from the pile as if she'd been waiting for them to arrive. "If you'll just go see the cashier and bring back a receipt, we can sign Mr. Cavanaugh out." She tapped the sheet clipped to the outside of the chart. "The doctor's left discharge papers and instructions."

Denise wet her lips. Now she *really* wished Will hadn't come along. This was going to be embarrassing enough as it was without having him witness it. "The cashier?"

"Yes, right downstairs." The nurse indicated the elevator behind them. "The office behind the Admitting desk."

Will could sense her tension. It wasn't hard to guess its source. "C'mon," he urged, taking her arm, "it won't take long."

She sighed, the fight temporarily drained out of her. "It will if they want to be paid in full before they release him."

He rang for the elevator. "They're not unreasonable. Some arrangement can be made."

* * *

The redheaded woman in the cashier's office sighed, looking at the chart before her. She re-read the admission sheet on the inside cover.

"No insurance, no permanent address." She looked up, directing her question to Will. "Who authorized this?"

"Doc Black." Will leaned over the desk. He'd gone to school with the woman. They'd shared the same dismal grade in World History. "Come on, Vera, Mr. Cavanaugh's already had the services and he and his daughter intend to pay the bill. You can come up with some kind of schedule of payments, can't you?" he coaxed. "You were always good in math."

"Better than you," she reminded him, looking at the printout again. The dubious frown refused to disappear. "I don't know, with no collateral..."

"We've got plenty of collateral," Denise interjected with just a touch of desperation coloring her indignation. "We have the carnival rides."

Not saying a word, Vera turned the bill around on her desk so that Denise could see the total.

Denise's heart sank as she stared at the astronomical figure. After surgery, her father had gone into the coronary care unit. And then the doctor had authorized a longer stay at the hospital to observe Tate in case something unexpected developed. That translated into a huge bill. There was no schedule of payments the hospital could come up with that would begin to dig her out from under the debt.

The solution that occurred to Denise was too drastic for her to cope with immediately. Yet there was no other option available.

Lifting her chin, she squared her shoulders as her eyes met the woman's. "We'll sell the rides. That'll cover the bill."

Will stared at her. He didn't know nearly as much as he would have wanted to about Denise, but there was one thing he was positive of—she loved the carnival rides. If she hadn't, he knew she would have left the road a long time ago.

"You don't mean that," Will said.

The last thing she wanted was sympathy, because sympathy was only pity in a fancy coat. Denise lashed out at him.

"Don't tell me what I mean," she snapped. "I said we didn't owe anyone and we're going to keep it that way. I'd sell the rides a dozen times over in exchange for my father's health."

"All right." Vera drew out another paper from her side drawer. "I just need you to sign this form about your intent to make proper restitution." She saw the question in Denise's eyes. "It's just a formality. The hospital likes to have everything documented."

"Fine." Denise ground the word out between her teeth as she signed.

"Is there someone you can sell the rides to?" It

didn't strike Will as the easiest thing in the world to undertake.

Having signed the papers, Denise could now hardly feel her legs as they walked out of the cashier's office. She looked down at the receipt in her curled fingers. Her father's ticket out. And their swan song.

She shrugged in reply, only half listening. "There's this organization that's been looking to buy us out. Zenith Rides. It likes to eliminate the competition," she said cryptically. "They'll pay for the rides."

He could see that this was killing her inside, but he knew that she'd never agree to accept a private loan from him. Her pride forbid it.

"Fair price?"

No, it wouldn't be, Denise thought. The organization knew they were down on their luck. They could smell blood.

But she didn't feel like going into that with him right now. "I don't have time to dicker."

Impatient, Denise punched the elevator button again. The steel gray doors remained closed, the bell silent. Where was the damn elevator?

"The form said you had six months," he said pointedly.

Did he think she couldn't read? She knew what it said. And it didn't make a difference. "Six months, six days, what does it matter? I'm not going to be able to come up with that kind of money anytime soon.''

Will's better judgment and discretion evaporated in the face of her unhappiness. "I could lend—"

She turned on him, her eyes bright with unshed tears just as the elevator finally arrived.

"Don't even say it. Don't even start. I am no one to you and you're not going to lend me anything.'' She almost flung herself into the elevator

She had a way of sapping his patience, Will thought, even if he understood her need for pride. He'd been there himself, in a place where there was nothing but pride to see you through. But it didn't have to be that way with her.

"Damn it, Denny, why don't you take down that stone wall you've built around you and let someone help you?"

"Because if I take down that stone wall—'' her voice almost broke ''—I haven't got anything to protect me.''

"From what?" he demanded.

"From you," she blurted out, then collected herself. "From being hurt again. And please, don't start talking to me about apples and orchards. That sounds very nice under a star-filled sky, but this is broad daylight and things look very different in broad daylight.''

He wasn't giving up, but he was tottering perilously close to the edge. "You're not headstrong, you're bullheaded.''

"Maybe," she allowed, "but I'm still around to tell the story."

"To who, Denny, to who?" he demanded. "You won't let anyone in close enough to listen."

Damn him, he was going to make her cry and she couldn't let her father see her crying. He had enough to deal with without worrying about her. "No one asked you to listen. Or to stay."

"For two cents, I'd—"

"You'd what?" she demanded, goading him. She didn't want charity, emotional or otherwise.

The elevator opened on the second floor. He strode out. "Nothing. I came along to help you bring your father to my parents' ranch and I'm bringing him to my parents' ranch." His parents had both insisted on it. "Now do us both a favor and stop talking before I'm tempted to strangle you."

She marched past him to her father's room. "Fine."

"Fine," he snapped back.

But it wasn't fine and they both knew it.

"You two can talk, you know." Sitting in the back seat, Tate looked from his daughter to Will. The silent tension in the car was thick enough to cut with a dull knife. "It was my heart they unclogged, not my ears."

Denise turned in her seat, trying to muster a smile for her father's benefit. Her heart ached so, she thought it was going to crack in half. "We just don't want to tire you out, Dad."

"Tire me out?" he scoffed. "I've been doing nothing but laying flat on my back in a hospital bed. I've got energy stored up to go dancing if I could find a willing partner."

Will welcomed the opportunity to make small talk. "You can ask my mother once I get you to the ranch."

Tate nodded. "It's very nice of your folks to put me up this way."

"They're glad to do it," Will assured him. "It'll give my mother a chance to fuss over someone who's not a blood relative. You might have noticed, she loves to fuss."

"I noticed. Wonderful woman, your mother." Tate chuckled softly, then looked at the back of his daughter's head. He recognized the tense set of her shoulders. "Denny, how are we paying for all this, the hospital, the operation?"

"We're managing." This time, she refused to turn around, afraid her father would read too much in her expression. He'd find out soon enough. For now, until the wheels were set in motion, she'd keep the truth from him. It was better for all of them that way. "Like always, Dad, we're managing."

10

The expression on Denise's face when he left her remained with Will all day and well into the next. At every turn, it gnawed at him like a ravenous shrew down to its last morsel of food. Like now, when he should be looking at the blueprints Drake had brought in for his review.

He knew she didn't want to sell the only source of livelihood she and her family had, yet there was no other way for her to pay off the hospital bill. Will supposed that on the bright side, the sale would give them a nice piece of change after all the bills were taken care of. There was a lot she could do with the money. Settle down for instance. But what would she do afterward? And would she be happy doing it?

Guaranteeing the happiness of this headstrong female had become very important to him.

Drake sighed as he rolled up the blueprints. By the way he blinked and looked up at him now, Drake doubted if Will had heard half of what he was saying.

"If I didn't know any better," Drake commented, patting the ends of the rolled-up paper, "I'd guess that our single-minded, ultrafocused Will Cutler was preoccupied."

He was more than preoccupied, he was in love. There was no question about it, no doubt. Like his brothers, he'd always known his own mind. The knowledge came to him with the form of a lightning bolt—swift, true and unchallenged. He loved her. Her resilience, her determination, her heart. Her.

Will sat up in his chair, suddenly alert as an idea began to form. An idea that had nothing to do with what Drake was saying. Will hated being inert when there was something to be done. Looking at Drake, he thought he knew what that something was.

"And you'd be right. Drake, your brother's on the city council, right?" Not waiting for an answer to the rhetorical question, Will surged ahead, "Does the town still want to build an amusement park?" he asked.

For a second Drake stared at his friend blankly. He shrugged. "You'd have to ask Hal, but it's one of the things on the council's back burner as far as I know." His eyes narrowed. "Why?"

Will turned his chair toward the computer on the side of his desk. He switched to an empty screen. His fingers immediately began to fly across the keyboard. "Because I just think I might have a deal that's going to make everyone happy."

Curious, Drake peered over Will's shoulder. "The boss included?"

"Yeah, the boss included," he answered without looking up. "Now I'd appreciate it if you'd go and let me do my work."

Drake saluted. "Your wish is my command. Send for me when you're ready to make sense."

But what was more important, Will thought as the door closed behind Drake, was that it would make Denise happy. Or at least, he amended silently, it should.

And if it didn't, he would.

Half an hour later, his notes and arguments printed out and laying on the desk in front of him, Will was on the phone, scrambling for backup. He had only one shot at this and he wanted to get it right.

"C'mon, Hank, you're the one with the gift for gab in the family. You're the one in the hotshot advertising firm, what do I do or say to make the town council members sit up and take notice?"

He heard Hank's deep laugh rumble in his ear. "You might try delivering the proposal without your shirt on and wearing your jeans one size too tight. According to Quint, two of the council members have had their eye on you for quite some time now."

Normally, he didn't mind shooting the breeze with Hank. He missed his brother since Hank had moved to Southern California, but he was short on time right now. "Very funny. I need help."

"Actually, for the first time in years, I'd say you didn't. You're finally acting like a normal male instead of the strong, silent patriarch dedicated to nothing but hard work and family."

The description fit him like a glove and Will didn't balk at it. There wasn't anything more important to him than his family and his career. There still wasn't. He just had his eye on expanding, that's all. "I don't have time to let you play talk show host with me, Hank. You're in advertising. How do I make sure I sell this concept to them?"

Hank thought for a minute. He'd been part of Serendipity all of his life and had the advantage of being able to look at the picture from two sides: that of a child and that of an enterprising adult.

"Remind them how people turn out to attend the carnival every year. Capitalize on the fact that if Serendipity had an amusement park on its outskirts, people from neighboring towns all over would come to spend their time and money here. Do a little of what you're good at, Will. Sketch in things that'll make the local shopkeepers start seeing dollar signs coming in instead of going out." Hank made a note to himself on his pad as ideas began to emerge. "Get their attention and maybe we can even launch a small ad campaign for you here, give the park statewide attention. If not, I'll see what I can come up with for you on my own," he promised, warming to the idea. "This has great potential, Will. If you hang around for a few more minutes, I'll fax you some preliminary ideas you can use on the council."

It was going to go well, Will thought. He could always tell. It was a feeling in his bones. "You've got it—and Hank?"

"Yeah?"

"Thanks."

Hank grinned to himself, glancing at the photograph of Fiona on his desk. Beside it was a small, personal calendar he kept apart from his work schedule. On it was a countdown of the days remaining until they were married. He'd never thought he'd look forward to settling down as much as he did.

"Don't mention it," Hank said. "I know what it's like."

For a second, Hank lost him. "You know what what's like?"

Receiver caught between his neck and shoulder, Hank typed in a few lines on his computer. "Walking five inches off the ground because some cute little lady's crossed your path."

"I think if I called her a cute little lady, she'd

hand my head to me." But for the most part, he figured Hank had a good grasp of the situation.

From all reports from home, Hank was willing to bet that his oldest brother had his hands full. "Doesn't matter what they do, as long as they take notice of you." He finished typing. "Okay, let me polish this a little and I'll send it over to you. Oh, and good luck," he added as an afterthought. "Not that, with my notes and your sketches and charm, you'll need it."

Will tried to feed on Hank's confidence. For the first time in his recollection, he felt a little nervous about a proposal. "Yeah."

But he would, Will thought a few minutes later as he dialed the mayor's number. He'd need luck— a great deal of luck. On a lot of fronts.

"Denise."

Denise turned around at the sound of his voice, damning herself that her pulse leaped at the mere thought of seeing Will again. Knee-deep in trouble and all she could clearly focus on was him.

Why was she doing this to herself? Why was she allowing this to happen all over again? Will, this feeling, all of it was ice cream, she thought, just ice cream. She couldn't make a steady diet of ice cream and eat it all her life. No one could, no matter how good it tasted.

But just this once, she could step off her diet just for a little while longer.

It would be gone all too soon. They were leaving at the end of the week. She tried not to think how much she'd miss him.

Shutting the toolbox on the ground with the point of her toe, she wiped the grease off her hands on the rag hooked to her belt. Stubbornly she waited for Will to come toward her rather than meeting him halfway.

"I was beginning to think you'd lost your taste for the carnival."

"No, I'm just acquiring it." Though his mind was full of his news, he paused a moment just to enjoy the way the sunlight caught in her hair. He touched it, feeling as if he'd captured a golden beam in his hand.

Denise wanted him to hold her, to make her feel safe and warm and unafraid. She knew it was impossible. Those kinds of things weren't wrapped up in a man's arms, waiting for delivery.

So instead, she stayed where she was, a cynical smile on her lips as she looked around the grounds. "Talk about bad timing—"

"Something wrong with the ride?" He nodded toward the carousel behind her.

She realized he was referring to the fact that she'd been working on it as he approached. "No, just upkeep. Always upkeep."

And sometimes it drained her. But what was she going to do without it? What was she going to do with her days when there was no Ferris wheel to check, no carousel horses to polish, no slides to erect?

No Will.

The future loomed before her, large and empty.

He nodded, letting go of the small talk. Excitement jumbled the words in his brain and he tried to sort them out. He'd been calmer presenting his idea to the council. Will had no idea why telling Denise about it made him feel uncertain. This was just what she'd want.

Wasn't it?

Denise studied his face. Something was up. "What's on your mind?"

Maybe if he'd brought his sketches with him— but he'd left them in the car. Taking a breath, he launched into it. "I've got some great news."

What was great news to one person wasn't particularly great to another, Denise thought. She knew better than to feel enthusiastic, but the feeling began to bubble within her anyway.

"All right, I'm listening."

"I've just talked to the town council and they want to buy your rides." Will watched her face, waiting for the relief, the excitement to take hold. All he saw was surprise and wariness.

She didn't follow him. Will had never even mentioned that Serendipity had any use for her rides after next week. What was he talking about?

"What?"

It was obvious that her enthusiasm, as with everything else about her, was slow to evolve. That was all right, Will was feeling enthusiastic enough for both of them.

"Yes, isn't it great? They want to build an amusement park right outside the town limits and they need rides. Your rides." The momentum in his voice built. "Not only that, but once the park is up and running, they'll need someone to manage rides and oversee—" He stopped. Far from happy, Denise looked upset and angry at the news. "What's the matter?"

She waved him back when he took a step toward her. The look in her eyes held him back as she tried to find the words.

There weren't any.

"Don't do this to me, Will."

It was his turn to feel lost. What did she mean, "to" her? He was doing this for her. For all of them. "Do what?"

She wasn't going to cry, she wasn't, though frustration almost wrung the tears from her. "Don't do this to make me grateful to you."

Will hadn't a clue why she said that. All he could guess was that somehow, it was leftover baggage from her relationship with Audra's father. Well, he meant for that baggage to be jettisoned over the middle of the ocean on a transatlantic flight as soon as was humanly possible.

Will took hold of her shoulders to force Denise to look at him instead of everywhere *but* at him. "I didn't do it to make you grateful to me, Denise. I did it to make you stay."

Shrugging, she broke free. Ever since David, she'd made her own way. Hers and Audra's. And her father's as well. She wasn't about to be beholden to any man. Ever.

"I already called Zenith Rides, they said they'll buy everything—lock, stock and barrel." Even as she said it, she felt something twist within her gut.

"But this is better," he argued.

How could she just turn her back on this? Will thought. He'd fought the fight of his life getting everyone to agree on it instead of tabling the matter indefinitely the way they customarily did. She couldn't just fling this back in his face now.

Denise spun on her heel to look at him. "Why? You don't know how much money they offered me."

She was doing everything she could to make him back away, but she wasn't going to succeed, damn it, he thought. He saw through her charade. Behind the bravado was a vulnerable woman who needed to be held once in a while. Who was human, just like the rest of them.

"This is better because we're not just offering you money, we're offering you a place to stay." He lowered his voice, coaxing her. "A place to set down roots."

But she knew better than that. "What you're so nobly offering me, Will Cutler, is a roller-coaster ride—straight over a cliff."

"Well, that's one ride you can scratch off the list," he quipped. "It eliminates repeaters, not to mention that maintenance would be a bear." He could see that she was afraid despite the fire in her eyes. Camouflage, all camouflage. "And just how do you figure it's straight over a cliff?"

"Because if I stay, I'm going to fall in love with you."

He smiled at her, a soft, gentle, disarming smile. So, she was afraid of falling in love. One of them was already there. "Would that be so bad?"

She fought to keep from being undone by it... By the look in his eyes. "Yes, it would. Because what do I do when you walk away?"

He passed his hand through her hair. Decades from now, he wanted to be able to look upon this face, to feel what he was feeling right at this moment. "Maybe I won't walk away."

Oh God, she was slipping fast. To keep focused, she dug her nails into the palms of her hand. "All right, run away then. Take a plane, a ship, a horse, a hunchback camel, I don't know, but you'll leave,'' she cried. "And then—"

He placed a finger to her lips to silence her. She jerked her head away. Gently, but with determination, he took her, struggling, into his arms.

"Stop it, Denise. I'm not going anywhere—unless you want me to."

Her chin shot up. "All right, go. Go! I want you to." But he continued to hold her and she could feel her resistance crumbling. "I want you to stop being so nice and wearing me down. I want you to stop making my daughter crazy about you. I want you to stop making me think that there's some kind of hope." Tears were glistening in her eyes. "Because there isn't."

He refused to let her go. Raw sympathy raked over his heat. "He must have done one hell of a job on you." And he could have killed David for it.

She was past lies. "He did."

For a long moment, Will studied her face, gauging his thoughts. "He wouldn't have if you hadn't let him."

Maybe it was true, but the observation stung anyway. Her eyes grew into angry slits. "That's why I'm not letting you in close."

He'd bet the next ten years of his life that they were discussing a moot point. She'd already let him get close. Just as close as he'd allowed her to get. "Want to know what I think?"

"No, I don't." She didn't want to hear any words that would weaken her already weakening resolve.

Will continued as if she hadn't said anything. "I think that you've already let me in close and now you're afraid—"

The word was like a red flag being waved in front of her. "I'm not afraid."

His gaze held hers, daring her to be honest. "Then why are you running?"

"I am not running," she insisted. "I'm just being sensible."

There was that word again. And it was a lie. Will's mouth curved. "Turning your back on love doesn't strike me as being very sensible."

She hated it when he smiled at her that way, as if he could read her mind and had robbed her of all her defenses. "Who said anything about love?"

"I just did." He shook his head, still holding her to him. "Boy, twenty-six and losing your hearing already. You better hang on to me, Denise. In a few short years I might be the best you could do."

In her heart, she knew he was the best she could do now or ever. The very best. But she was so afraid that it wouldn't last. That she would be hurt again and this time, there would be no pieces to pick up. Because if she loved him, if she gave her heart to him, she wouldn't hold back, not even the tiniest piece.

Denise was aware of blinking back tears. "What did you just say about love?"

Gotcha, he thought, pleased. "Oh, so now you want details?"

"Yes." She forced the word out between gritted teeth. "I want details."

His lips softly played along hers, nipping just a little. "Ask me nicely."

He'd almost succeeded in melting her completely, but Denise didn't have to let him know that. A woman had to hold on to some of her secrets, some of her dignity, even when she was in love. "I'm not separating your head from your shoulders, am I?"

He laughed. "Guess 'nice' is a relative term." And then the laughter died in his throat. Will smiled into her eyes. "I love you, Denise, despite the fact that you seem to love arguing more than anything else on the face of this earth."

"That's not true—"

He grinned, vindicated. "I rest my case. So what do you say? You said you had to sell the rides to pay your father's expenses. Why not sell them to the town council and insure your future as well? It's not charity." He second-guessed her objection before it was voiced. "They'll need someone who's experienced. There'll be work for the crew members who've stayed on with you as well. Cecil and Skip, Roy..." He let his voice trail off.

She bit her lip, torn. Wanting desperately to say

yes, but still hesitant. She was leading with her heart. The last time she'd done that, she'd paid dearly.

"Zenith might give you a better price, but we can give you the better deal." His lips whispered another kiss along hers. "A place to stay."

Her heart was hammering so hard, it hurt. "They're throwing in a house?"

He'd won, he thought. But he knew better than to let her see that he knew.

"No, but I will. I'll build a house for you and Audra and your father," he promised. "There's a little plot of land just outside of town that's just been begging to have something erected on it. As it happens, it's not too far away from where they plan to have the amusement park. What do you say?"

She pretended to hold out. Denise already knew what she was going to say. "I've never had a house before."

He couldn't imagine not ever having a roof over your head to call your own. "Never?"

Denise shook her head slowly. "Never."

He gathered her closer. "Then it's high time you had one. A Will Cutler special. And while we're at it, have you ever had a husband before?"

She stared at him, afraid that she hadn't heard him correctly. "No," she breathed.

The grin was from ear to ear. "Then it's high time you had one of those, too."

"A Will Cutler special?" she asked.

"You read my mind. Now read my heart." Placing her hand over it, he looked into her eyes.

It was beating as hard as hers. The realization instantly erased all the doubts she'd had plaguing her. "What am I supposed to see?"

"That there's only one name on it. Yours."

She needed to hear the words, to know that she wasn't just dreaming this. "Are you asking me to marry you?"

"The only way I know how. Stay, Denise. Let me build that house for you."

She threw her arms around his neck. "For us," she said, correcting him. "Build that house for us, Will—on one condition."

He cocked his head. "Which is?"

"That you call me Denny."

He'd made it to the inner circle, he thought with no small amount of relief. "Then it's yes?"

He was right, she could read his soul in his eyes. "If you're serious, it is."

"I am."

Her smile was broad and warm. "Then it is. C'mon, let's go tell Audra."

But he didn't release his hold on her. "Wait."

She searched his eyes for a telltale sign. "Cold feet?"

Slowly he moved his head from side to side, his eyes on her mouth. "Hot blood."

"Oh." For the first time, he saw laughter in her eyes. "Okay."

And as he kissed her, Denise felt herself being swept away again. And for once, she didn't resist. She had a very strong feeling that she was never going to have to resist again.

* * * * *

The saga of the Cutler family continues
with THE LAW AND GINNY MARLOW,
coming in January only in
Silhouette Yours Truly.

Take 2 bestselling love stories FREE

Plus get a FREE surprise gift!

Special Limited-Time Offer

Mail to Silhouette Reader Service™

3010 Walden Avenue
P.O. Box 1867
Buffalo, N.Y. 14269-1867

YES! Please send me 2 free Silhouette Yours Truly™ novels and my free surprise gift. Then send me 4 brand-new novels every other month, which I will receive months before they appear in bookstores. Bill me at the low price of $2.90 each plus 25¢ delivery and applicable sales tax, if any.* That's the complete price, and a saving of over 10% off the cover prices—quite a bargain! I understand that accepting the books and gift places me under no obligation ever to buy any books. I can always return a shipment and cancel at any time. Even if I never buy another book from Silhouette, the 2 free books and the surprise gift are mine to keep forever.

201 SEN CH72

Name	(PLEASE PRINT)
Address	Apt. No.
City	State	Zip

This offer is limited to one order per household and not valid to present Silhouette Yours Truly™ subscribers. *Terms and prices are subject to change without notice. Sales tax applicable in N.Y.

USYT-98   ©1996 Harlequin Enterprises Limited

For a limited time, Harlequin and Silhouette have an offer you just can't refuse.

In November and December 1998:

BUY **ANY** TWO HARLEQUIN
OR SILHOUETTE BOOKS and

SAVE $10.00

off future purchases

OR BUY ANY THREE HARLEQUIN OR SILHOUETTE BOOKS
AND **SAVE $20.00** OFF FUTURE PURCHASES!

(each coupon is good for $1.00 off the purchase of two
Harlequin or Silhouette books)

JUST BUY 2 HARLEQUIN OR SILHOUETTE BOOKS, SEND US YOUR
NAME, ADDRESS AND 2 PROOFS OF PURCHASE (CASH REGISTER
RECEIPTS) AND HARLEQUIN WILL SEND YOU A COUPON BOOKLET
WORTH **$10.00 OFF** FUTURE PURCHASES OF HARLEQUIN OR
SILHOUETTE BOOKS IN 1999. SEND US 3 PROOFS OF PURCHASE AND
WE WILL SEND YOU 2 COUPON BOOKLETS WITH A TOTAL SAVING OF
$20.00. (ALLOW 4-6 WEEKS DELIVERY) OFFER EXPIRES
DECEMBER 31, 1998.

I accept your offer! Please send me a coupon booklet(s), to:

NAME: _____

ADDRESS: _____

CITY: _____ STATE/PROV.: _____ POSTAL/ZIP CODE: _____

Send your name and address, along with your cash register
receipts for proofs of purchase, to:

In the U.S.	In Canada
Harlequin Books	Harlequin Books
P.O. Box 9057	P.O. Box 622
Buffalo, NY	Fort Erie, Ontario
14269	L2A 5X3

PHQ4982

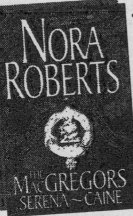

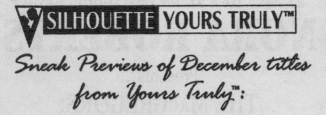

SILHOUETTE YOURS TRULY™

Sneak Previews of December titles from Yours Truly™:

A HUSBAND FOR CHRISTMAS
by Jo Ann Algermissen

Beautiful Barbara Stone refused to be any man's Christmas bonus! When she saw "December 24 SIR weds SEC" scribbled across Sam Isaiah Reed's desk calendar, she knew exactly who the groom would be, but S-E-C? Could it be short for secretary...his secretary...*her?* Marrying her boss was unthinkable!

When it came to Sam, er, Mr. Reed, she had only professional thoughts of conference calls, computers and...kisses at his credenza. Maybe marriage by memorandum *was* in her future!

SECRET AGENT SANTA
by Linda Lewis

Secret agent Zachary Steele was what you could call *overqualified* to be tough boss Chloe Betancourt's assistant. He was sharpening pencils and fetching coffee with hands registered as deadly weapons. But he couldn't blow his secret agent cover—nor could he romance his lovely boss-from-hell. Still, Zachary knew the dragon-lady act was *her* cover, and underneath the power suit was a woman ready to experience the power of love. Perhaps it was time to show her a Christmas to remember.